BORN TO RUN

A Shadowrun™ Novel

STEPHEN KENSON

A ROC BOOK

ROC
Published by New American Library, a division of
Penguin Group (USA) Inc., 375 Hudson Street,
New York, New York 10014, USA
Penguin Group (Canada), 90 Eglinton Avenue East, Suite 700, Toronto,
Ontario M4P 2Y3, Canada (a division of Pearson Penguin Canada Inc.)
Penguin Books Ltd., 80 Strand, London WC2R 0RL, England
Penguin Ireland, 25 St. Stephen's Green, Dublin 2,
Ireland (a division of Penguin Books Ltd.)
Penguin Group (Australia), 250 Camberwell Road, Camberwell, Victoria 3124,
Australia (a division of Pearson Australia Group Pty. Ltd.)
Penguin Books India Pvt. Ltd., 11 Community Centre, Panchsheel Park,
New Delhi - 110 017, India
Penguin Group (NZ), cnr Airborne and Rosedale Roads, Albany,
Auckland 1310, New Zealand (a division of Pearson New Zealand Ltd.)
Penguin Books (South Africa) (Pty.) Ltd., 24 Sturdee Avenue,
Rosebank, Johannesburg 2196, South Africa

Penguin Books Ltd., Registered Offices:
80 Strand, London WC2R 0RL, England

First published by Roc, an imprint of New American Library,
a division of Penguin Group (USA) Inc.

First Printing, November 2005
10 9 8 7 6 5 4 3 2 1

PUBLISHER'S NOTE
This is a work of fiction. Names, characters, places, and incidents either are
the product of the author's imagination or are used fictitiously, and any
resemblance to actual persons, living or dead, business establishments,
events, or locales is entirely coincidental.
   The publisher does not have any control over and does not assume any
responsibility for author or third-party Web sites or their content.

If you purchased this book without a cover you should be aware that this
book is stolen property. It was reported as "unsold and destroyed" to the
publisher and neither the author nor the publisher has received any payment for this "stripped book."

The scanning, uploading, and distribution of this book via the Internet or
via any other means without the permission of the publisher is illegal and
punishable by law. Please purchase only authorized electronic editions, and
do not participate in or encourage electronic piracy of copyrighted materials.
Your support of the author's rights is appreciated.

To my friends, family,
and Christopher, most of all

ACKNOWLEDGMENTS

Thanks to Janna Silverstein for getting the ball rolling and to Sharon Turner Mulvihill for picking it up and running with it. You're two of the best editors I've had the pleasure to work with. Thanks to Mike Mulvihill for his invaluable advice on all things Shadowrun, and to everyone involved with the Shadowrun Duels game and the creation of Kellan and her associates.

TRANS-POLAR
ALEUT

ATHABASKAN
COUNCIL

SALISH-
SHIDHE
COUNCIL

QUÉBEC

ALGONKIAN-MANITOU
COUNCIL

Seattle

TIR
TAIRNGIRE

SIOUX
NATION

UNITED CANADIAN
AND AMERICAN
STATES (U.C.A.S.)

UTE
NATION

Denver

CALIFORNIA
FREE STATE

PUEBLO
CORPORATE
COUNCIL

CONFEDERATED
AMERICAN STATES

AZTLAN

CARIBBEAN LEAGUE

NORTH AMERICA
AS OF 2060

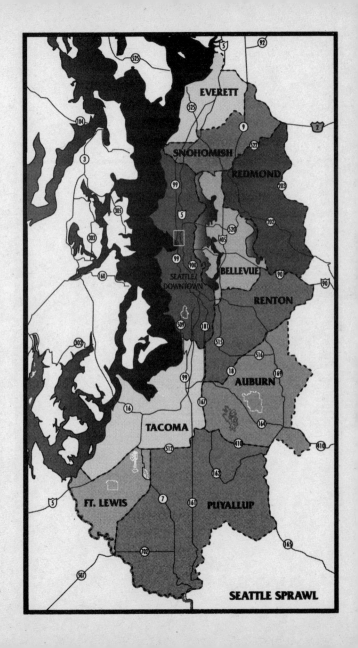

SEATTLE SPRAWL

1

When Kellan Colt reached the Underworld, it started to rain. Not very much, just a drizzle from the leaden clouds, which were lit from beneath by the neon glow of the metroplex, spattering droplets of light across the grimy windows of the Grid-Cab.

"Thank you for choosing Grid-Cab, Ms. Webley," the onboard computer chirped cheerfully as Kellan removed her credstick from the slot, her balance now a few nuyen lighter than she would have liked. The cab door hissed open automatically and Kellan climbed out. Someone else was waiting to climb in and the cab chirped, "Thank you for choosing Grid-Cab, please slot your credstick and enter your desired destination. . . ."

Kellan looked up at the kromeglow marquees that

climbed the walls to loom overhead, spelling out UN-DERWORLD 93. The building was a converted warehouse: huge, blocky and made of gray plasticrete, pocked with scars and chips and liberally decorated with graffiti, which only added to its character as a fixture of the Seattle nightclub scene. The line to get in already extended down the block, made up mostly of eager young corp-babies dressed up in their latest street-wear for an exciting night of slumming oh-so-close to the Puyallup Barrens, their idea of life on the edge. Mixed in were the locals, their clothes not quite so perfectly coordinated, their "look" not so practiced. Kellan spotted a couple of dwarves, a few elves looking like they'd just stepped off the runway of a fashion show, even some orks and a troll dressed in leathers and torn synthdenim.

She ignored it all, jammed her hands into the pockets of her leather jacket and jandered right up past the head of the line like she belonged there, eyes straight ahead, chin up.

A massive hand grabbed her arm and spun her around.

"Hey, where do you, think you're going, little girl?" The deep voice carried over the noise of the crowd and the pounding beat of the music pouring out from inside the club.

Kellan looked up into one of the ugliest faces she'd ever seen. He was an ork, which meant he stood

2

head and shoulders above Kellan, above most humans, in fact. His face was straight out of a scary children's story: a broad nose and jaw, sloped brow and white tusks jutting up over his upper lip. His skin was dark and dotted with warts and his brown hair hung in heavy dreadlocks, decorated with shiny bits of metal. His outfit was sharp enough to shave with. He wore a white shirt that strained to contain the bulging muscles of his arms, shoulders and broad chest, and a close-fitting dark vest. His pants were tailored (they had to have been to fit him at all well) and his boots were worn but high quality. She could see that the outfit wasn't brand new, but it was put together in a way that showed the ork (or his employer) had taste, and some cred.

Kellan shook off the ork's hand and drew herself up to her full height, which still left her staring at the middle of his chest, and met his stare with one of her own.

"I'm going inside," she said, putting as much frost into her voice as she could manage.

"How old are you, kid?" the bouncer scoffed. Kellan heard a few jeers from the line, but ignored them, keeping her focus on the bouncer.

"Twenty-one," she replied without missing a beat.

"Let's see some ID."

Kellan produced her credstick and handed it to the bouncer, who slotted it into the portable reader clipped to his belt. Before she handed it over, Kellan keyed the stick to slip the ork some cred, if he wanted it.

"I'm here on business," she said, just loud enough for the ork to hear. His eyes flicked from the display on the screen of the reader to her face and back without any sign of emotion, then he tapped the screen a couple times.

"Oh yeah? What kind of business?" he asked casually, not looking up.

Her initial response was, "None of yours," but she bit that down. There was no point in hacking off the big ork. No real point in lying to him, either.

"I'm looking for someone," she said. "A chummer named G-Dogg." *That* got him to look up.

"Why?" the ork asked with a smile. "He owe you money or something?"

"Like I said, it's business. He around?"

The ork shrugged. "Haven't seen him, but G-Dogg hits a lot of clubs." He took the credstick out of the reader and handed it back to her. "If I see him I'll let him know that you're looking for him, Miz Webley. Have a good time." He waved her on toward the door of the club.

"Thanks," Kellan said. The ork turned back toward the line, where the next pair of club-kids were loudly protesting his decision to let her cut the line.

"All right, next!" he said. "Let's see some ID."

Kellan walked through the front doors and entered the Underworld.

The first thing that struck her was the sound, a wall of noise coming from the towering amps flanking the broad stage. Flashing lasers pulsed in time to the beat, and a montage of video clips splashed across the floor-to-ceiling screens along the back wall.

Beyond the lobby, a broad staircase curved around the crowded dance floor off to the side of the stage. A band was wailing out tunes at a volume that seemed to make the rafters shake, and the crowd responded with enthusiastic moshing. Her eyes were immediately drawn to the elf fronting the band; his natural charisma made him a perfect lead singer. And she was not surprised to see a sasquatch backup vocalist, since their ability to imitate any sound practically guaranteed they'd end up in the entertainment industry. She'd never actually seen one live before.

Standing in the doorway, Kellan sighed as the light and the noise enveloped her. She'd made it. Of course, her attitude and a decent fake ID, along with some well-placed tips, had gotten her into more than a few clubs back home in Kansas City, but this was fragging *Seattle*. It was the big time. The Seattle Metroplex was a happening place, a little slice of the United Canadian American States out in the midst of the potentially hostile Native American Nations, right near the elven nation of Tir Tairngire and the California Free State. Gateway to the Pacific Rim, where the shadows were deep and dark, and there were chances at big scores, not the small-time biz of Kansas City.

"Seattle . . ." Kellan breathed, looking around the club and just taking it all in. The place was jammed with people, most of them dressed in the latest club fashions, all of them gyrating to the music.

Kellan considered the contrast between her clothes and what everyone else was wearing. She wore a beat-up leather jacket over a white T-shirt that hadn't been washed in quite some time, tucked into some old jeans that were a little too big for her and cinched at the waist with a secondhand belt, and heavy work boots on her feet. Obviously, what she lacked in style, she made up in attitude. After all, she was in, and the fashionable were still waiting.

Unconsciously, one hand reached up to brush across the jade amulet she wore on a heavy gold chain around her neck. It was by far the most extravagant element of Kellan's outfit. She still wasn't quite used to its weight, but it felt so *right* around her neck. From the moment she'd seen it she'd known that it was meant for her. She just wished she knew more about it. Hopefully, that was one of the things she would find out in Seattle.

It had been in a package that had just shown up at her aunt's one day. It was a lucky thing Kellan had actually been home at the time, or she was sure that her aunt would have pawned the contents and she'd never even have known it existed. Her aunt would have used the money to buy some cheap liquor, to help her forget about all the money she'd shelled out for Kellan's care over the years. Which she never let Kellan forget: she was constantly harping on how Kellan was nothing but a burden to her ever since her mother had left her there.

There was no return address on the package, but the postmark showed that it was shipped from Seattle. Inside, Kellan found the amulet and a few other things: a stun baton, a tightly folded armored vest, some grenades, a survival kit, a certified credstick with a balance of a few thousand nuyen, and a computer-printed note. "This stuff belonged to your mother. Thought you might want it."

There was no signature, no indication of who might have sent it, but Kellan was smart enough to grab an opportunity when she saw it. She packed up her few possessions and got the hell out of her aunt's place within a week. She was finished with being told that she was nothing but a burden, when she was paying most of the bills. She was fed up with the service jobs where privileged corp-kids sneered at her or, worse yet, treated her like she didn't exist.

She swore to herself that she wasn't going to end up like her aunt, working in some dead-end job, struggling to make ends meet, and pouring what little nuyen she had left over into getting drunk so she didn't have to think about what a waste her life had become.

Kellan was going to make something of herself. That mean earning some cred, and for an undereducated kid with no legit prospects, there were only two ways to do that; selling herself on the streets, or working in the shadows. She had no intention of doing the former, and with the gear that came in the package, Kellan had enough of a stake to get a start as a shadowrunner.

She proved herself on a couple of runs in Kansas City and earned enough to supplement the nuyen she had and make some connections to get to Seattle, where the package had come from, where the real action was. Now she was here.

Lost in her thoughts, Kellan nearly walked into a guy standing at the railing above the dance floor. She turned, prepared to apologize or defend herself, but it wasn't necessary. She saw the vacant stare and the narrow cable that snaked from the chrome jack behind the guy's ear down to the little box he wore at his belt. He was a chip-head, living in a virtual world of recorded simsense played directly into his brain. He swayed and shuffled in a slow sort of dance that had nothing to do with the music in the club, lost in his digital fantasy. Kellan jammed her hands back into her pockets and resolved to pay attention. Enough thinking about the past. Kansas City was behind her. She was in Seattle now, and it was time to see if she could get down to business.

Off to the side of the dance floor was a crowded cluster of tiny tables and chairs made by dwarves with a sense of humor. A crowd pressed in all around them, and Kellan wove her way through toward the bar that curved along the side wall. As she angled her body to slide between two scantily clad orks, a strange figure near one end of the bar captured her attention.

It was a ten-meter-tall statue finished in chromed metal that looked vaguely like a Buddha, with a bald, bullet-shaped head and a big belly swathed in a long, belted robe, with sandals on its bare feet. Loops of neolux tubing were wrapped around the statue's arms and legs and a speaker in its belly blasted out the sound from the stage. The look on the statue's face wasn't the serene expression Kellan associated with Buddha statues, though. It was simultaneously sly and stern, as if the fellow was in on some secret joke. As Kellan watched, puffs of smoke jetted from around the statue's feet, catching the laser light from the scaffolding above. Glowing words played across the chrome surface, appearing and disappearing so quickly that they were almost subliminal. They slid across the shining metal, proclaiming, QUESTION AUTHORITY, 93, and LOVE IS THE LAW.

"Don't stare for too long," a voice cut through the noise. "The Beast has been known to hypnotize newbies who stare."

Kellan turned back toward the bar and realized she was standing right next to it. She had managed to make it through the rest of the crowd while entranced by the sight of the statue. An elf stood behind the bar, leaning a bit toward her, hands resting on the countertop, one holding a rag he was using to wipe it down. Like every elf Kellan had ever seen, he looked like a simstar: tall and handsome, his straight black hair worn shoulder length and tucked behind his pointed ears. He gave her a dazzling smile and tapped the bar in front of him.

"What'll it be?"

Kellan slid her credstick into the reader on the bar and tapped the display screen.

"How about a beer and something on the side?" she asked.

The elf kept smiling and raised one delicate eyebrow. "Sure thing. The beer is five nuyen, but the chaser will cost you fifty."

Kellan tapped the screen. "Done. You know a chummer called G-Dogg?"

Up went the eyebrow again. "Yeah, I know him. Why are you looking for him?"

"Business," Kellan replied curtly. "Is he here?"

He shrugged expressively. "I don't know. Haven't seen him around tonight, but G-Dogg is a busy guy, you know? He works a lot of clubs: Penumbra, Dante's Inferno. He might show up later on, or he might not."

Kellan suppressed a sigh. "Okay. Well, can you tell him I'm looking for him?" she asked. She tapped a few more keys on the screen, shooting her contact info to the bar's comp. "That's my number."

"Sure thing," the bartender said. He set an open bottle on the bar and popped a chip into the comp's port, tapping the screen to transfer her contact info. Kellan withdrew her credstick, and the elf removed the datachip and slipped it into his pocket as Kellan picked up her drink.

"If you need anything else," he said, "just holler."

"Thanks."

Kellan tasted her beer. It wasn't bad, but Kellan wasn't there to drink. She was there on business, but how was she supposed to get anything done if she couldn't even make a decent contact? She caught herself then, realizing that she was still thinking like a KC runner. Seattle's shadow community was huge—she shouldn't expect to find her target the first place she looked.

She'd come to the Underworld because she'd heard that G-Dogg was the man to talk to for a shadowrunner new to the Seattle scene; that he knew things and people who could set up an initial contact. Kellan's hand closed around the credstick in her pocket. The balance was getting pretty low. She needed to score some work, and soon, or else she was going to be back out on the streets. She didn't even have enough money left for a return trip to Kansas City—not that she ever planned on going back there. She was going to make it in Seattle no matter what, but to do that she needed to hook up with the right people.

That was when a troll lurched out of the crowd around the tables, looked around for a moment then focused on Kellan like a heat-seeker.

He was big and ugly, and made the bouncer out front look handsome by comparison. His head was low and squat, almost football shaped, with downward-curving horns on either side and one protruding tusk broken and capped with chrome. His domed head was shaved down to dark stubble and his big, pointed ears held numerous heavy metal rings. So did his bushy eyebrows and his broad, flat nose, which had a ring through it, like a bull. He wore a heavy leather jacket draped with chains from the shoulders.

"Hey, baby, haven't seen you around here before," he slurred in a deep, gravelly voice. He stood nearly three meters tall. Kellan looked him square in his stomach, a slight paunch that protruded over a wide, black leather belt. Even with the distance between them, his breath was strong enough to knock down a wall. He reeked like a brewery and staggered slightly, like he'd just drunk one.

"And you won't again," Kellan said, pushing away from the bar and leaving her beer there, barely touched. A massive, leather-clad arm blocked her way.

"Where you goin'?" the troll said. "You haven't even told me your name. I'm Horse." He smiled, showing her a mouthful of yellowed, broken teeth, and bobbed his head in an exaggerated nod, winking at her. "That's right, honey, it means just what you think."

"Yeah?" Kellan asked. "Well, maybe you should find yourself a nice centaur or something."

"Huh?" the troll grunted, grabbing for her arm. "Don't be that way, baby. I just wanna—*urk!*" He stopped short when Kellan snapped her stun baton up between his legs.

"That big enough for you, *baby?*" she said. " 'Cause I'm betting that it's more than what you've got. Now, unless you take your hand off me right now, drekhead, they're going to change your name from Horse to Mare."

"Fraggin' smoothie slitch . . ." the troll muttered,

one hand balling up into a fist. Kellan squeezed the trigger. There was a sizzling crack and the troll howled on an impossibly high note, barely audible above the pounding music, then fell like a massive tree. He lay there, twitching, as Kellan backed away a few steps. She heard a smattering of applause and a few approving hoots from women in the crowd next to the bar, then she turned and stalked back toward the entrance. People cleared out of her way, though only the clubbers closest to the bar even noticed the big troll rolling around on the floor groaning.

The ork bouncer at the door noticed Kellan as she headed out.

"Hey," he said. "Have any luck?"

"Yeah, all bad," Kellan replied, jamming her hands into her pockets. The drizzle had turned into a steady rain, drumming on the street, seriously dampening the spirits of most of the wannabes still waiting in line. Kellan strode past the line, pulling her phone out of her pocket to call another Grid-Cab. She thought about hitting another club, but she really just wanted to give it up and go somewhere warm and dry to crash.

She heard a commotion back toward the club entrance and looked back to see Horse and two other trolls outside, looking around the darkened street.

Horse was yelling. Then he spotted Kellan, grabbed his buddy's arm and pointed.

"Oh, drek," Kellan said. Then she turned and ran as the three of them came charging after her.

She ran as fast as she could, dodging around people on the street, but the three metahumans coming after her moved fast despite their massive size, and they clearly knew the area better than she did. She cut left into the first alley she found, hoping to lose them, only to discover a heavy chain-link fence blocking the end of it. She hit the fence at a run and started to climb, but it was slick from the rain and her boots weren't made to grab the mesh of the fence. She slipped when she was only halfway up, and a heavy hand grabbed the back of her jacket, dragging her down.

Kellan wriggled out of the jacket and dropped to the ground, leaving the big troll holding nothing but a handful of synthetic leather. Horse slammed into her, pinning her back against the cold, wet metal of the fence, his reeking breath in her face, his bulk making the mesh dig painfully into her skin. Kellan's stun baton was in the pocket of her jacket, out of reach, along with anything else she could use as a weapon.

The troll smiled evilly and grabbed Kellan's chin with one massive paw, twisting her head so their faces were mere centimeters apart. Rain dripped from his bushy brows and face as he ran his tongue along his tusk.

"You're not going to be so pretty after we're done with you, baby," he growled, "but if you just relax, you might enjoy it."

2

"**N**ow we're going to have some fun," the troll grinned.

"Hey!" yelled a familiar voice from the end of the alley. "Back off!"

As the trolls turned to look at the intruder, Kellan could see it was the ork bouncer from the nightclub striding down the alley toward them, cracking his knuckles. He carried no weapons that she could see.

"I said back off," he repeated.

"Frag you!" Horse shot back over his shoulder, and his two chummers stood between him and Kellan and the bouncer.

"Bring it on, then," the bouncer invited, and the two trolls rushed him.

The first troll to reach the bouncer wore his thick blond hair in a buzz cut. He swung a massive fist the size of Kellan's head, but the ork ducked low in a blur of motion, spun around and hit Buzz Cut in the lower back with his fists, sending the bigger metahuman stumbling forward onto one knee in a pile of trash, cursing in pain.

The other troll, who had a heavy scar running across his pockmarked face, took a swing at the ork. The bouncer blocked the punch, nailing Scar with a kick to the stomach that made the troll double over and let the ork deliver a knee to Scar's face. There was a crunching noise and a spout of blood from the troll's broken nose as he stumbled back.

Then Buzz Cut got back to his feet and grabbed the bouncer from behind. He wrapped his massive arms around the ork's torso, lifting him off the ground. The troll's massive shoulders and biceps flexed as he squeezed, and the ork bouncer struggled in his grip.

Scar wiped blood from his face and shook his head, then reached into his leather jacket. There was a loud snap as he flipped open a heavy knife and advanced on the pinned bouncer.

Held tightly in the troll's grip, the ork smashed a booted foot into the bigger metahuman's knee, causing Buzz Cut to howl in pain and drop him just as Scar rushed in. He dropped below the swing of the knife then dove forward to tackle Scar, and the two of them tumbled into a pile of garbage.

"Finish him off, you fraggers!" Horse yelled impatiently as Buzz Cut shuffled toward the melee again.

Kellan kicked at Horse and immediately regretted it. For a moment, he had almost forgotten about her, but her kick missed its intended target and smacked him in the thigh, reminding him of the girl he had pinned against the fence.

He backhanded Kellan, sending her sprawling onto the wet pavement, and she tried to scramble to her feet before he could grab her again. Horse raised a hand in front of his face and short, chromed blades like scalpels popped out of his blunt fingertips. Behind him, Kellan saw Buzz Cut stumble back, clutching one arm and cursing, as Horse took a step toward her.

"I'm gonna cut you good, slitch," he said, grabbing the front of Kellan's shirt and hauling her up to her feet as his other hand swung back.

It was like time stopped for a moment, as Kellan brought up her hand in a futile attempt to fend off the razors at the tips of Horse's fingers. She felt a flush of heat, the pounding of her heart in her chest. A reddish haze obscured her vision, focused entirely on the troll in front of her. The jade amulet at her neck felt cold against her burning skin. Kellan saw her outstretched hand glow red and she could see the black shadows of the bones through her flesh. Then heat seemed to rush out of her like a wave.

There was a whooshing sound, and the troll burst into flames.

Horse's clothing, even his leather jacket, caught fire, instantly transforming him into a blazing torch. The troll screamed, dropped Kellan and began rushing about, trying in vain to put out the flames. He dropped to the ground where he rolled and kicked as his screams and the smell of burning cloth, leather, hair and flesh filled the alley.

The fight came to a standstill when Horse ignited, but the ork bouncer was quick to take advantage of the situation. While the trolls stared in horrified fascination at their chummer, the bouncer delivered a kick to the chest of Scar that sent him stumbling hard into the wall. His knife clattered somewhere in the alley as the troll slid down the wall and into a heap on the ground.

Buzz Cut looked from the ork bouncer to his chummers, one lying out cold, the other still smoldering and moaning in pain, then he slowly backed a few steps toward the open end of the alley, turned and ran.

Kellan slumped against the chain-link fence, staring in shock at the smoldering form of Horse, his clothing and flesh charred. It was like all of her energy had left her in a rush and she suddenly felt cold and very, very tired. She dropped down onto the ground as the ork bouncer came over to her and, when she glanced down, she noticed her hands were shaking violently.

"Kid. Hey, kid. . . ." A voice was calling from far away. She looked up to see the bouncer standing over her with a concerned expression on his ugly face. Kellan saw him as if at the end of a long, dark tunnel. Her vision started to swim.

"Hey, are you okay?" he asked. Then everything went dim, and Kellan passed out.

When Kellan came to, she was lying on a cot in a small, dim room, with a scratchy old UCAS army-issue blanket thrown over her. She flipped it off and swung her feet onto the floor. She immediately regretted moving, as a dull ache began pounding behind her eyes, emphasizing the bass beat of the music coming through the walls. She leaned forward against her knees, massaging her temples to try to make the pain go away.

Then she did a reflexive pat-down of her gear, to make sure it was all there. She sighed in relief. Nothing had been touched, as far as she could tell. Even her jacket was draped over a nearby chair. She rested her hands on the edge of the cot, allowing her eyes to grow accustomed to the dimness and the throbbing in her head to ease somewhat.

Multicolored light flooded into the room as the door opened enough to admit a shadowy figure. Kellan jumped to her feet, immediately reaching for her stun baton.

"Hey, hey!" the gravelly voice said. "Chill! It's frosty, kid. It's just me." When he took a step forward, Kellan could make out the features of the ork bouncer. She slumped back down onto the cot as he made his way over.

"How're you feeling?" he asked, flipping a chair around and straddling it so he could lean on the back of it.

"Like I got run over," Kellan said. "How long have I . . . ?"

"About an hour," the ork replied. "It's a little after 2300."

Kellan shook her head slowly and massaged her forehead with one hand.

"Coulda been a lot worse," the ork told her.

"Yeah," she said slowly glancing up at him. "Thanks. I appreciate the help."

"Null sheen," the ork said with a tilt of his head. "But I wouldn't have been so fast on the draw if I'd known you were packin' mojo."

"What—what do you mean?"

"That trick where you turned ol' Horse into a matchstick," he said. "Nasty."

"But I—I didn't do that," Kellan said. Had she? She recalled the sensation of heat right before the troll caught fire.

"No? Well, it sure wasn't me," the ork retorted. "The way I saw that fancy necklace of yours kind of glimmer, and the way you were so tired out, I figured for sure it was you. So you're not a spell-slinger?"

"Me? No, I mean, I've never . . . I've never been able to before. . . ." Kellan's hand went almost involuntarily to the amulet, recalling how it had almost burned with cold against her skin. Now it was comfortably warm. Then she remembered her hand, glowing red-hot, and the shadows of the bones showing through the skin. She held it in her other hand, but both looked completely normal now. She glanced up at the bouncer and touched the amulet.

"You said that this . . . glowed?"

The ork shrugged. "Well, not exactly glowed, but kinda shimmered a bit. I've seen stuff like that around magic types before an' figured you must be one of them, too. Is that thing magical?"

"I don't know," Kellan said. "I just got it recently. It belonged to my mother."

"Well, maybe that's got something to do with it," he said, scratching the back of his head with a couple of blunt fingers. "I dunno. I know magic when I see it, but I don't know much about how it works." Then he looked at Kellan again, this time like he was seeing something new.

"You know, if you're not a magician, then it wasn't

a real smart thing you did, going up against those three Spikes. Horse and his chummers, they're bad news. No place for a newbie to be messing around."

"Who says I'm a newbie?" Kellan bristled.

"Well, I haven't seen you around here," he countered, "and you didn't know to leave well enough alone, or at least make sure that Horse stayed down for the count the first time you tangled with him."

"*He* decided to mess with me," Kellan shot back. "And I handled myself just fine."

"Well, yeah, until you ran into that alley."

Kellan bit back a retort, letting it out as a sigh. "I guess you're right. Sorry. I do appreciate your help."

"Like I said, null sheen. Gave me an excuse for some roughhouse, and I've been looking for some of that all day." He gave her a broad grin that showed off his tusks, and Kellan couldn't help but laugh.

"You *are* new in town, though, aren't you?" he asked pointedly. "What's your name?"

"Kellan Colt," she said. She stopped short for a second, realizing that she had given the ork her real name instead of the fake name on her credstick. If he noticed, he didn't show it.

"Where are you from, Kellan?"

"Kansas City," Kellan replied. "I just got here yesterday. I'm working on making some connections to find work."

"How long were you working the shadows in KC?" he asked.

"Two years."

"That's a pretty long time, but Kansas City isn't Seattle, kid. Things are different around here."

"Yeah, I'm getting that idea," Kellan said.

The door opened and the elf bartender stepped in. He handed Kellan a plastic cup of water and a small slap-patch.

"Here," he said. "This should help fix you up." He nodded toward the patch when Kellan just looked at it. "It's for your head." Kellan read the label, then peeled the patch off its backing and stuck it on the side of her neck over the artery, where the pain relievers could work their way quickly into her bloodstream. Then she took a long sip of the cool water.

"Thanks," she said, and the elf nodded.

"Yeah, thanks, Leif," the ork echoed as the bartender headed for the door.

"Anytime, G," he said, closing the door behind him.

Kellan's head whipped around so fast she almost dislodged the slap-patch.

"You're G-Dogg!" she said to the bouncer, who just nodded.

"Yup."

"Why the frag didn't you say so?"

"Because I didn't know you from any other wannabe off the streets, kid, and because you obviously didn't know me or you wouldn't have been asking me. I told you, this ain't Kansas no more. You're in Seattle now, and things are different here in the plex. If you don't get introduced by somebody, then you're nobody. That's the way it is."

"Why didn't anyone else say anything?"

"Because they know me here and they know well enough to keep quiet. Leif knew that you must have walked right past me when you came in, but obviously you didn't know who I was. He figured that if I didn't speak up, I had a good reason, and I did."

"So you were just playing me," Kellan said, her eyes hard.

"No, I was watching you. I wanted to see how you handled yourself, what your angle was, before I decided to talk to you."

"And?" Kellan asked.

"From what I saw, you handle yourself pretty well, kid. You need to learn a few things about life and the shadows in Seattle, but I think you can do okay for yourself. 'Sides, spell-slingers aren't that easy to come by, even around here."

"I told you—"

"Yeah, I know, you're not, and you don't know what that thing does. Tell you what. If you're interested, I think I know somebody who might be able

26

to come up with answers to both. I don't know much about magic, but Lothan, he knows everything there is to know, and he'll probably tell you so. That is, if you're up for it."

When G-Dogg grinned again Kellan gave him a tight-lipped smile in return.

"What the hell?" she said. "Let's go."

3

G-Dogg escorted Kellan to a beat-up Honda-Kia Argent parked in the fenced lot behind the Underworld. The car chirped and the lights flashed as they approached, though Kellan didn't see G-Dogg take out a remote control. The ork went around to the driver's side and Kellan climbed into the passenger side. The interior of the car was cleaner than Kellan expected and, when G-Dogg punched in the ignition code, the engine thrummed to life with barely restrained power.

"Nice, ain't she?" the ork said with a measure of pride.

"Yeah, nice," Kellan said, though truthfully she wasn't all that impressed.

"She may not look like much," G-Dogg said, as if answering Kellan's unspoken thought, "but, like they say, she's paid for, and she's got it where it counts. It ain't all about flash, right?"

G-Dogg picked up Route 167, following it north toward the district of Renton, where they merged onto I-405. Along the way, he pointed out different places that he knew, giving Kellan a running travelogue of the sights. In particular, he mentioned the Shadow Lake Correctional Facility, making a point of the fact that he'd never been inside himself, but that he knew more than a few people who had.

"Over that way is Knight Errant's main training facility for the whole Pacific Northwest," he said, gesturing toward the sprawl of lights stretching away from the highway.

"They do a lot of the security work in Seattle?" Kellan asked. Knight Errant was a subsidiary of the megacorporation Ares Macrotechnology, and well known as one of the top-flight security contractors in the biz.

"Not as much as they want to be doing," G-Dogg said with a snort. "All the megacorps maintain their own security forces, naturally, and the police services contract for the metroplex belongs to Lone Star, so Knight Errant is limited to handling mostly Ares security and a lot of comparatively small stuff. They've been gunning to take the metroplex services contract away from Lone Star for years." Lone Star Security Services out of Texas was well known to Kellan, and to any shadowrunner. They provided more contracted police services than any other corporation.

"K-E's got a shot at it again this year," the ork continued. "But odds are the Star will hold on to the contract. They've got the mayor in their pocket, so it's a lock provided they don't frag things up so badly that ol' Mayor Lindstrom has to ditch them for damage control."

The roar of engines sounded from behind them and G-Dogg glanced into the rearview mirror.

"Hang on," he said to Kellan, and then he floored the accelerator so hard that Kellan was slammed back into her seat. The Argent shot forward with a whine from its engine and G-Dogg cut the wheel, swerving into the far-left lane. There was little traffic on the highway so late at night, but G-Dogg still had to dodge around a couple of cars and one drone truck making its way northward, driven by its onboard dog-brain and guided by the metroplex's Grid-Guide computers.

Kellan glanced back over the seat to see a cluster of single headlights behind them, about half a dozen or so motorcycles keeping pace with their car.

"Who are they?" she asked.

"Hellhounds," G-Dogg said curtly. Then he swerved the car to the right, dodging around a Ford American that blared its horn at them, the sound quickly trailing off as they blasted past.

Even though G-Dogg slammed on the brakes, they hit the off-ramp so fast that Kellan was sure the ork was going to roll the car. But the Argent dropped back onto all four wheels with a squeal of tires and G-Dogg slowed down a bit as the motorcycles roared past the exit, continuing north on the highway.

"Friends of yours?" Kellan asked the ork and G-Dogg just grinned.

"As if. The Hellhounds claim 405 as their turf, and the Hounds are all norms, humans. They don't much like seeing metahumans in their territory, so I try and stay out of their way, just in case they're bored or something."

He smoothly merged onto I-90, heading west toward the glittering towers of downtown Seattle in the distance.

"So why cut through their turf, then?" Kellan asked. "I mean, we're kind of going the long way around, aren't we?"

"Not really," the ork replied. "I-5 belongs to your new chummers the Spikes. They're a go-gang, all trolls like your chummer Horse, all on fraggin' huge bikes. The Spikes are touchy at the best of times, but lately they're likely to frag anything that comes through their territory. They've come into some new ordnance lately, and they're probably none too friendly towards us right now. The Hounds are a lot easier to avoid."

Kellan thought about the trolls that G-Dogg had fought outside the Underworld. Then she imagined an entire gang of them, mounted on Harleys and armed to the teeth.

"I see what you mean," she said.

The glittering cityscape parted before them as the highway stretched out over Lake Washington toward a heavily wooded island.

"That's Council Island," G-Dogg said as they cruised toward it. "It's the Native American Nations embassy in the plex, but the tribal council lets traffic cross I-90 with no hassle, as long as you aren't looking to get off the highway late at night." The ork eased up on the gas a bit as they approached the island, either to make sure he was observing the speed limit or to allow Kellan a better look, or both.

She took in the traditional-style Salish longhouses with the tall, carved totem poles standing out front, surrounded by thick stands of trees. She also noticed the heavy ferrocrete blockhouses at the checkpoints off the highway, manned by stern-faced Native soldiers wearing fatigues accented by feathers and beadwork that contrasted with the modern assault rifles slung over their shoulders. She thought that she saw a Salish shaman at one of the checkpoints, wearing a bearskin cloak and a bone necklace.

It was the shamans who had secured the future of their people and the Native American Nations. The

Ghost Dance War between the Sovereign American Indian Movement and the United States and Canadian governments had been fought in 2017 and won with magic, not long after the Awakening brought magic back into the world. The Native Americans were among the first people to recognize that their ancient traditions suddenly had real power, and they were willing to use it.

At first it seemed like a joke: ragtag bands of Indian terrorists up against the most powerful military on Earth. Then the Ghost Dancers unleashed the power of the four largest volcanoes in the Cascade Range simultaneously. There was no fighting against the power of Mother Nature, so the nations of North America were forced to negotiate with the Indians.

Nearly half of North America was ceded to the new Native American Nations, but the Seattle Metroplex remained a part of what was now the United Canadian American States, situated in the midst of the Salish-Sidhe Council, one of the strongest members of the NAN. Council Island, in turn, was surrounded by UCAS territory, one nested inside the other, with everyone keeping a close eye on everyone else.

Kellan refocused on the present as G-Dogg exited toward downtown Seattle, the heart of the metroplex.

"So, who's this guy we're going to see?" she asked G-Dogg. The ork chuckled evilly.

"Oh, I think you should just wait and see," he said. "Some things, and some people, just can't be explained. You have to see them for yourself. Lothan is one of those."

G-Dogg navigated expertly through the streets of downtown Seattle to the Capitol Hill neighborhood. Like most people who grew up on the flat plains of the midwestern UCAS, Kellan was surprised by the hills in this part of the city. The area was strictly middle lifestyle: row houses and restored Victorians along with small storefronts, coffeehouses and places catering to the *shaikujin*, "straight citizens" with honest, decent-paying jobs. Kellan wondered who someone like G-Dogg could possibly know in this kind of neighborhood.

The ork bouncer found a parking spot, muttered a pleased-sounding, "parking karma strikes again," deftly maneuvered the Argent into it, then killed the engine and gestured at the house just ahead of them. It had a turret on one side and a broad porch stretched around the front. The drapes were drawn and the looming windows stared out onto the street like dark eyes.

"That's it," he said, getting out of the car. Kellan followed him up the stairs to the house's front door, which featured a brass knocker shaped like the head of a gargoyle.

G-Dogg smiled mischievously. "After you," he said,

gesturing toward the door. Kellan wondered what sort of game the ork was playing, but she would be damned if she was going to take the bait. She reached out to grab the brass handle and knock on the door.

Before her hand even touched it, the door swung open silently and Kellan nearly jumped out of her skin. A glowing spot of light, about the size of a softball, appeared in the air at eye level and bobbed there, shedding a golden glow like a disembodied torch.

"He's expecting us," G-Dogg said, as if that explained something. The ball of light drifted slowly away from the door and then paused, as if waiting for them. Kellan looked from it to G-Dogg and back again, then stepped across the threshold and into the house, followed closely by the ork. The door swung closed behind them with a quiet click as the ball of light bobbed down the hall.

The interior of the house was quiet, and lit only by the glowing sphere. Very little light came through the heavy drapes covering the windows, even though there was a streetlight directly across from the house. The sphere passed through an open doorway at the end of the hall and disappeared, so Kellan followed it.

The room beyond seemed fairly large, though it was difficult to judge the size, given the clutter it contained. Every available bit of wall space was covered with shelves, each containing more books than Kellan had seen in her entire life. Not dataslates or flatscreens, but actual, honest to God, dead-tree *books*, printed on paper with bindings of leather and cloth, stamped with gold and silver, some of the titles too faded to read in the dim light. In and around the books were scattered all sorts of trinkets and bric-a-brac: a crystal ball, a gnarled wooden wand decorated with feathers, strings of beads, dried flowers, half-melted candles, odd-shaped rocks, a silver goblet or two. A horned skull grinned from a top shelf. The air was musty and thick with the smell of old paper, dust and the faint spice of dried herbs and rose petals.

"Well then, G-Dogg," a voice rumbled. "What is it you've brought me this time?"

Kellan turned as the sphere of light drifted across the room to illuminate a large, shadowy figure seated beside a desk near the window. He was a troll, though not like any troll Kellan had seen before. Even sitting down, it was clear that he was huge; his curved horns probably brushed perilously close to the high ceilings in the house when he stood. His hair was thick and iron gray and he had bushy eyebrows that drew together over his dark eyes. His features were as craggy as if they had been roughly carved from stone, and his skin was greenish-gray.

He held open a broad, flat palm and the little light settled into it like a well-heeled pet. Its gleam highlighted the golden symbols running down the edges of the open robe he wore over a dark shirt and pants. An amulet of gold and gemstones rested against his barrel chest. Those dark eyes looked Kellan over, assessing, appraising.

"Kellan," G-Dogg said, "this is Lothan the Wise—"

"Master of mysticism, arch-arcanist, and initiate of the inner mysteries," the troll interjected, rising from his seat. He cast the ball of light up toward the ceiling where it hovered, shedding its glow on the room, and bent to scoop up one of Kellan's hands in his own, bowing and bringing it to his lips. "At your service. And you are . . . ?"

"Um, Kellan . . . Kellan Colt," she managed to reply, and the troll allowed himself a small smile.

"Welcome to my humble abode, Kellan Colt," Lothan said, gesturing to the room around him. "Please, make yourself comfortable." He stood aside so Kellan could reach the red settee wedged under the window. Stacks of papers and books that had obviously occupied it before their arrival now surrounded it.

"Thanks," she replied. G-Dogg made himself comfortable on the settee next to her, squeezing Kellan off to one side, while Lothan settled back into his broad chair.

"My friend G-Dogg told me only a little about you when he called," the troll said. "He said that you displayed some skill in the arts arcane of late."

"Huh?" Kellan said, glancing at G-Dogg.

"He means the way you flash-fried Horse, kid."

"Oh. Well, like I told G-Dogg, I don't know how that happened."

"So you have no previous experience with magic?" Lothan asked.

Kellan shook her head. "Not really. I mean, I learned a little about it in school, the Awakening and all that, and I knew this guy in Kansas City who was a shaman—"

Lothan cut off the recitation by holding up a hand. "But no previous *personal* experience with magic?" he asked.

Kellan shook her head again.

"Hmmm," the troll rumbled, stroking his chin. He sat back and slowly looked Kellan over from head to toe and back again, scrutinizing her carefully. Kellan felt her skin crawl. There was just something unsettling about the way the troll looked at her.

"Um, Lothan—?" she began, but G-Dogg shushed her.

"Quiet kid," he whispered. "He's working."

If Lothan noticed the exchange, he chose to ignore it. A moment later, he glanced up at Kellan, his eyes seeming to come back into focus.

"Would you mind if I examined that trinket around your neck for a moment?"

Kellan's hand immediately went to the amulet.

"No, I guess not," she said. She lifted off the chain and held out the necklace to Lothan, who plucked it from her hand and gently turned it over, his thick fingers surprising her with their dexterity. His eyes took on the same unfocused look as he examined the amulet from every angle, gently waving one hand in the air around it, as if he was feeling something invisible all around the jade jewelry. For a moment, Kellan saw one shaggy gray eyebrow raise in a quizzical expression. Then Lothan raised his head once more and held the necklace out to Kellan, who took it from him and started to put it back on.

"Wait a moment," the troll said. "Please hand that to G-Dogg." The ork nodded reassuringly, and Kellan did as Lothan asked.

"Now then," the troll said, in an authoritative voice, like a professor lecturing a class, "close your eyes." Kellan hesitated and he added, "Please." When Kellan complied, he continued. "I want you to picture in your mind a sort of egg around your body, made of glass or crystal. It can be whatever color you want, but I want you to picture it as clearly as you can."

Kellan concentrated on imagining what Lothan described. She saw the crystalline egg shape as sort of pinkish, glowing like it was made of light.

"Do you have the image?" he asked and Kellan nodded.

"Good, good," the troll purred. "Just relax and keep concentrating on that image. Make the egg as smooth and perfect as possible."

Kellan sighed and focused on the egg image. She was starting to wonder what sort of nut-job this Lothan character was. Why was he having her imagine pretty shapes? She would have preferred him to offer some help in looking for work.

Suddenly, there was a flare of greenish light in her mind's eye. Kellan felt it strike against the pink crystalline egg like a sharp blow and pain flared behind her temples like someone had stabbed her in the brain with an ice pick.

"Ow!" she yelled, pressing the heels of her hands against the sides of her head.

"You okay?" G-Dogg asked, leaning in toward her. Kellan warded him off with an outstretched arm.

"Yeah, yeah, I'm all right," she said. "Just got a headache."

"Actually, what you have is a modestly effective spell defense," Lothan said.

"What?" Kellan asked. The troll mage looked extremely satisfied with himself, which Kellan began to suspect was his normal state of being.

"Spell defense," he reiterated. "The image I asked you to focus on is a basic exercise for reinforcing the aura and protecting against hostile spells. While you concentrated on it, I cast a simple stun spell at you and—"

"You what?" Kellan said, jumping to her feet.

"A stun spell," Lothan said, waving Kellan to sit back down. "Nothing permanently harmful. Indeed, all it should have done is put you painlessly to sleep."

"If that's your idea of painless, chummer, then—"

"If you'll allow me to *explain*. . . ." the troll mage said sternly, and Kellan stopped in midsentence. She closed her mouth and sat down with deliberate slowness.

"That's better," Lothan breathed. "Now then, as I was saying. My stun spell should have put you painlessly to sleep. Any mundane would have been out like a light. You, however, are no mundane, my dear." When Kellan just gaped at him, he continued. "You have some magical talent, albeit somewhat limited, and quite untrained. You're a magician."

"A . . . but how?" Kellan stammered. "I mean, if I was, wouldn't I know it by now?"

"Not necessarily. For some, the Talent emerges later in life. It may lie dormant until something activates it: stress, powerful emotion, even contact with other magic—something like that amulet of yours, for example."

"What about it?" Kellan said.

"It is most definitely enchanted," Lothan replied, furrowing his brow and stroking his chin, "although I have to admit that the exact nature of its enchantment eludes me. I've never seen anything exactly like it. Where did you get it?"

"It used to belong to my mother," Kellan said, "but I don't know where she got it. I—I don't know much about her, actually. I was hoping to find out more here in Seattle."

"Your mother, you say," Lothan replied. "Hmmm. Well, I certainly haven't seen the likes of this before. Perhaps it will yield some clues about her."

"Do you think?" Kellan asked.

"I make no promise, but it's possible."

"Well, you've got great news, kid," G-Dogg said, patting Kellan on the back. "You're a spell-slinger! You shouldn't have any trouble getting biz."

"She's *not* a trained magician, G-Dogg," Lothan interjected. "Just a raw talent with little else to back it up. She needs training. In fact . . ." Both Kellan and G-Dogg looked at the troll mage as he rolled his eyes in thought. Then he looked at Kellan.

"You intrigue me, my dear," he said. "I haven't seen a newly Awakened talent around here in quite some time—not one that wasn't already influenced by some pirate street grimoire or, worse yet, some corporate thaumaturgy program. Too many bad habits for them to break, but you, you're the proverbial tabula rasa, a blank slate. Plus, there's that intriguing amulet of yours." He wagged a finger in Kellan's direction, touching it to his lips briefly as he collected his thoughts.

"I'll tell you what," he said. "I would be willing to take you on as my apprentice, to train you in the arcane arts, teach you to harness and mold the potential that you have discovered, in exchange for certain considerations from you."

"What kind of 'considerations'?" Kellan asked cautiously.

"A percentage of your take, of course," Lothan said. "You would be working for me, in effect. If you're interested in shadow work, that is."

Kellan resisted the urge to glance over at G-Dogg, to see what he thought of Lothan's offer. That was something an uncertain newbie would do, not a seasoned shadowrunner. If she wanted to make it in the Seattle shadows, she needed to start handling things like this on her own, making her own deals. She deliberately paused for a moment to think it over, not taking her eyes off of Lothan, doing her best to size up the old troll and his intentions. Lothan's face was as unreadable as craggy stone, but really, he did seem to know his stuff, and G-Dogg said so, too, so what did she have to lose?

"Deal," Kellan said, extending a hand. Lothan

grasped it in his own massive paw and shook it firmly.

"Well, then," he said, "you can get started right away. I actually have a business meeting to attend this evening. G-Dogg, I'd like you to come along too, since this job might be something of interest to you. If all goes well, there are a few people I'd like you to call." The ork nodded in acknowledgment and Lothan slapped his knees as he levered himself up out of his chair and reached for a carved wooden staff resting against the nearest bookcase.

"Let's do business, shall we?" he said.

4

The place Lothan took them to was called Ebey's Bar. Lothan said that it was a pun when it came to doing business, but Kellan didn't get the joke. It sure as drek didn't look to her like the kind of place where shadowrunners cut deals. It was nothing compared to the glamour and glitz of Underworld 93 or some of the metroplex's other nightspots. It was just a run-down little hole-in-the-wall in Everett, wedged between two taller buildings. The inside was dim and smoky, decorated in dark-stained wood that created pools of shadow around the booths and small tables. The dull yellow lights over the bar barely succeeded in a feeble attempt at illuminating it.

Ebey's boasted a smattering of patrons at the tables and booths, no more than a dozen or so all told. At first glance, Kellan thought that the man behind the bar was an ork. He was certainly tall and broad enough, and ugly enough, but he lacked the tusks and pointed ears. His shaved head shone in the lights as he poured foaming beer expertly into mugs and slid them across the bar to a couple of guys wearing synthdenim and street leathers. The bartender glanced up as Lothan, Kellan and G-Dogg entered the bar. He exchanged an almost imperceptible nod with Lothan, then glanced toward the back of the establishment.

"This way," Lothan said quietly, taking the lead. The big troll made his way around the bar and between some of the tables toward the back, where two men waited at a table. Kellan noted there was no one else sitting near them, and the men sat where they had their backs toward the wall and a clear view of the front and rear entrances of the bar.

Kellan gave the two a quick once-over. The first man was clearly the one they'd come to see. He was younger than Kellan expected, although age was always difficult to tell with cosmetic surgery, magic and gene-cleansing therapy available to people with the money to pay for it. He was human, his dark hair cut in a fairly severe, almost military style, wearing a nondescript pair of black jeans and a burgundy sweater that was bulky enough to conceal ballistic padding, maybe a weapon or two. He also wore black leather gloves, meaning that he was probably a SINner, someone with a System Identification Number. His fingerprints, genetic map and other data were on the Matrix in some government computer somewhere. That meant he had to be especially careful not to leave traces behind. Shadowrunners like Kellan and G-Dogg didn't have SINs—at least not the kind you got from a government computer. They were blanks, ghosts in the machine, which was why SINners hired them in the first place. Shadowrunners who knew their business were careful to stay out of the databases of the governments and the corporations, since it was their anonymity—and deniability—that made them so useful.

Kellan wondered for a moment if the man was with the military. He certainly looked the part, and it wouldn't be the first time that the UCAS military (or those of other nations) had dealt with shadowrunners. He looked the three of them over with an appraising eye, but showed no signs that he was nervous, concerned or anything other than in complete control of the situation. Some of that confidence might have stemmed from the presence of the person sitting next to him.

The other man was an elf. Looking at him, Kellan wondered briefly if all elves looked like fashion models fresh from an image shoot. He looked young, too, but then all elves did, even the ones born at the very start of the Awakening some fifty years ago. He was tall and slender, but Kellan could see that his T-shirt with its Celtic-knot design was stretched across a well-muscled chest. His hair was auburn and shoulder length, a popular style with elves. He wore it pulled back into a ponytail. His eyes were vividly green. The elf's outfit didn't match the slick and understated style of the other man. Instead, he wore a heavy black leather biker jacket with chrome zippers and buckles, close-fitting T-shirt, torn blue jeans and black, knee-high leather boots. Kellan also noticed his studded black gloves were fingerless, and that he wore a sword in a scabbard across his back, with the hilt protruding above his right shoulder so he could draw it overhand. It still surprised her when she saw someone carrying a sword, though she knew that some dangers in the Sixth World were best handled with man-powered steel rather than modern weaponry.

"Mr. Johnson, I presume?" Lothan asked and the first man nodded, gesturing to the other chairs at the table. Lothan took the one directly opposite their contact, and Kellan and G-Dogg sat to either side of the troll mage, putting Kellan closest to the elf, who glared across the table at all of them.

Lothan didn't offer introductions, nor did Mr. Johnson ask for any. That wasn't his real name, of course. Shadowrunners referred to their employers as "Mr. Johnson" (or "Ms. Johnson," as the case may be) because anonymity and discretion was of paramount importance to shadowrunners, and to those who hired them. Potential employers didn't want their real names known in case something went wrong. What the shadowrunners didn't know, they couldn't reveal to the authorities, nor could they use it to attempt blackmail. Shadowrunners used street names for much the same reason.

"Let's get down to business, shall we?" Mr. Johnson said in a neutral, somewhat bored tone of voice.

"By all means," Lothan replied.

"Certain parties that I represent are interested in acquiring a particular shipment that is coming into the metroplex. I can provide information about the route the shipment will take into the plex. I need someone to acquire the shipment and deliver it to a location elsewhere in the metroplex that I will specify."

"And to whom does this shipment belong?" Lothan asked. Mr. Johnson shook his head slightly.

"I'm not prepared to discuss that until we have an agreement," he said. "The job pays forty thousand nuyen in certified credit upon completion and successful delivery of the goods."

"How soon does the run need to take place?" Lothan asked.

"Within the week."

"That's not much time," the troll mused aloud.

"Fifty thousand, with half up front and the remainder upon delivery."

"Forty-five, with five thousand in advance for expenses, and the other forty when you deliver."

Lothan paused for a moment. "Done."

"One other thing," Mr. Johnson said. "I want Orion here on the team," he tilted his head in the direction of the elf.

"I choose my own team," Lothan replied.

"It's part of the deal. Either take it or leave it," the Johnson said flatly.

"If we're taking him on, that's an additional expense," Lothan began.

"I don't want your fraggin' money," Orion growled from the other side of the table. Mr. Johnson placed his gloved hand on the table in front of the elf, silencing him.

"A separate arrangement has already been made," he told Lothan. "The payment for the job is for you and whomever you choose to hire. Orion doesn't need to be considered in your allocations." When Lothan studied the elf and then looked back at the Johnson, he continued. "That's the offer. Do we have a deal?"

"Make it eight thousand up front and, yes, we have a deal."

"Done," the Johnson replied. He reached slowly into a pocket on the sleeve of his sweater and removed a small palm computer. He tapped the screen a couple of times, then pulled a datastick out of the port and slid it across the table toward Lothan, lifting and withdrawing his gloved hand with deliberate slowness.

"That contains your advance and the information on the shipment time and route," he said. "The shipment belongs to Ares Macrotechnology and is coming into the metroplex by truck in a few days. It also specifies where and when you're to deliver the goods."

Lothan picked up the data stick and casually handed it to G-Dogg, who removed a similar pocket comp from his jacket and slotted the stick, glancing over the display and tapping the screen a couple of times. Then he looked up at Lothan and nodded.

"And if we need to contact you?" Lothan asked Mr. Johnson.

"Our only other contact will be at the prearranged meeting," he said. "You shouldn't need any contact with me beyond that. I trust you can handle this matter on your own."

"Of course," Lothan replied briskly. "Well, then, I believe our business is concluded."

The Johnson nodded and stood up from the table. "I'll be looking forward to our next meeting."

"Pleasure doing business with you," Lothan said. Then the dark-clad man departed, leaving the shadowrunners sitting at the table. The elf, Orion, stayed where he was as their new employer left, watching the others with a wary eye.

"You waiting for a tip, kid?" G-Dogg said to the elf.

"No," he said in a haughty tone. "I'm waiting to get started."

"Well, then, I suggest that you wait elsewhere," Lothan said. "We'll contact you when your services are needed."

"Your employer said that I'm supposed to be involved in this run," Orion said, placing one hand flat on the table and leaning forward for emphasis. Kellan tensed, waiting for the elf to jump to his feet.

"And you will be," Lothan replied, "but when and where I say. If you are going to be in on this, then the first thing you need to understand is that I call the shots. Now then, I assume that you have a means by which we can contact you?"

The troll and the elf locked eyes across the table and Orion was silent for a long moment. Kellan could see the tension in the line of his jaw and across his shoulders. Then the elf pulled the front of his jacket open with one hand and reached slowly into the front pocket with the other. Kellan could see that he was wearing a gun in a shoulder rig underneath, although his hand stayed well away from it. He pulled out a compact phone and G-Dogg responded by setting his pocket comp on the table. Orion tapped a code into the phone and beamed something to the pocket comp, which chirped.

"You have my number," he announced, pocketing the phone again. Then he rose from the table, turned on his heel, and swept out of the bar. Kellan noticed that G-Dogg turned to watch him go, but Lothan didn't, showing only his back to the elf's exit. A moment later they heard the roar of a motorcycle engine starting up and Kellan allowed herself to breathe again.

"That guy's gonna be trouble," G-Dogg said to no one in particular.

"I can deal with him," Lothan said with a dismissive wave of his hand. "It won't be a problem."

"I don't know," the ork replied. "Did you see the back of his jacket? The Ancients aren't people I want to tangle with."

"You're welcome to opt out if you want."

"Didn't say that. I just think that it could get messy if the Ancients are involved."

"Who are the Ancients?" Kellan asked, and the two turned toward her like they'd forgotten she was there. Kellan took note of the incredulous look on Lothan's face.

"They're a gang," G-Dogg said. "An elven gang, one of the biggest in the plex. The Ancients have chapters all over the UCAS, but there are a lot of them in Seattle because it's so close to Tir Tairngire. I would have said they were the toughest gang in the plex before the Spikes started moving in on their territory—now it's probably a toss-up. Not getting along with the Spikes is something you and our new chummer there have in common," he told Kellan with a grin.

"So that was the gang's symbol?" Kellan referred to the circled "A" in acid-green paint emblazoned on the back of Orion's jacket.

"Yup," G-Dogg said.

"Why would the Johnson want us to work with a member of a gang?"

"It's of no importance," Lothan interrupted tersely before G-Dogg could reply. "So long as Mr. Johnson's credit is good, it's none of our concern. He wants the elf involved with the run, so he will be, and this is not the place to be discussing it at any rate." He gave Kellan a meaningful look and she clammed up, stung by the implication about her lack of professionalism. Then the troll mage stood, putting an end to the conversation.

Kellan felt a hot flush of embarrassment and stood up quickly to follow Lothan and G-Dogg out of the bar. *Stupid*, she thought, *asking questions like some dumb kid!* She noticed how quickly Lothan and G-Dogg had frozen out Orion. Was that how they looked at her? Some kid that they were saddled with whether they liked it or not? Lothan *had* invited her along to the meeting, even if he didn't say two words to her about it, and G-Dogg didn't seem to think her questions were out of line, but . . .

But nothing, Kellan thought as she settled into her seat in the car. *I'm going to show them that I can do the job. This is the chance I wanted. I'm* not *going to frag it up.*

They went back to Lothan's place, where the troll mage excused himself for a moment to make a few calls, leaving G-Dogg and Kellan waiting in his cluttered study. When Lothan returned, he seemed satisfied with the results of his inquiries.

"G-Dogg, I'll want you to get in touch with a few people. I'll let you know the particulars soon."

"Okay," the ork said, getting to his feet. Seeing this, Kellan did the same.

"As for you," the troll said to Kellan, "we can start your instruction soon, provided that you're still interested. . . ."

Kellan nodded. "Yeah, count me in."

"Excellent," Lothan said with a nod. "Well, then, if you'll excuse me, I'm not as suited for these late-night rendezvous as I used to be, and there're still things to be done. G-Dogg, I'll contact you soon. You can show yourselves out."

"A'right, Lothan. See you later," the ork said. He paused for Kellan to precede him out the door, following close behind.

They didn't speak until they were in G-Dogg's car, on their way back toward Lake Washington.

"Hey, I just wanted to say thanks," Kellan said quietly.

"For what?" the ork replied.

"Well, for everything. Helping me out back at the club, getting me set up with Lothan—everything."

The ork chuckled. "Don't thank me yet, kid. You haven't started lessons with the 'master of the arts arcane,' yet." G-Dogg did an uncanny imitation of Lothan's lofty and educated tone of voice. "Don't get me wrong," he said, catching a look of concern on Kellan's face. "Lothan's a great mage—maybe even as great as he thinks he is. He really knows his stuff but . . . well, let's just say that he's not a real people person."

"Not like you," Kellan said.

"Nope," G-Dogg replied. "Sometimes I think it's because Lothan wasn't born a trog." Kellan was surprised, both by the information and G-Dogg's casual use of a racial slur usually hurled at orks and trolls by Humanis Policlub supremacists.

"He wasn't?" she asked.

"Nope. Lothan was born *before* the Awakening, kid. He's older than you and me put together. He's been around the block more than a few times, and he's still here to talk about it."

"So he wasn't always a mage, either?" Kellan said.

"Well, just about," the ork replied, shifting gears and changing lanes to dodge around some slower-moving traffic. "Ol' Lothan was like eleven or twelve when the Awakening hit, so he was just a kid. I dunno whether his Talent woke up then or if it was when he goblinized."

"Wow," Kellan said. "I just figured he was maybe forty or so."

"Well, he looks it, if he was born a troll. Hell, if Lothan was born a troll, he'd be dead by now. Not too many trolls make it to his age."

Or orks, Kellan thought. While elves born at the dawn of the Awakening were still young and vital well into their fifties and sixties, those born as orks and trolls weren't blessed with similarly long life-spans. In fact, the so-called goblinized metahumans physically matured faster than humans, and they aged faster, too. Orks were lucky if they lived past forty or so, and a troll who reached fifty was practically ancient. Apparently, metahumans born as humans were different, living out their normal human lifespans. G-Dogg said that he was born an ork. Kellan suddenly realized G-Dogg was probably younger than she thought.

"Me, I'm glad that I didn't have to go through the

change," G-Dogg mused aloud. "I've heard that it hurts like nobody's business."

Kellan shuddered as she imagined muscle and bone reshaping itself in response to some hidden genetic directive, warping the normal human form into that of an ork or troll. By itself, the process of adding all the additional body mass had to be incredibly painful, even if it was all magic. No wonder some of the first orks and trolls had gone insane from the process. She thought about Lothan going though that, turning from a human into a troll over the course of several pain-wracked days, and felt a sudden sympathy for the old mage.

"I hope I can learn how to do it all," Kellan said.

"What, magic?" G-Dogg asked. "Beats the frag out of me, kid. I'm a total mundane. Never got the mojo, and that's fine with me. Too complicated. I like to keep things simple. I think you'll do okay, though. Aren't too many runners in the plex who know magic better than Lothan."

"So," the ork said, changing the subject, "you got a place to crash? 'Cause if you need one, you're welcome to check out my doss." He glanced at Kellan briefly before returning his eyes to the road.

"No thanks," she said. "I've got a place. I just need to pick up my ride at the club."

"No problem," G-Dogg said in a carefully neutral

tone. "I've got to go back there to take care of some stuff anyway. I'll drop you off."

The trip back to Underworld 93 was less eventful than the trip downtown. G-Dogg made occasional small talk about places Kellan should check out in Seattle, but didn't say anything more about Lothan or the run. In fact, Kellan noticed that the ork didn't say a thing about the job or what he thought about Mr. Johnson or the elf ganger Orion. Kellan didn't bring it up either, concerned about coming off looking like a newbie again.

Then they were outside the club. The line of wannabes was gone and the night's business was winding down, though Kellan could still hear the pounding beat of the music from inside. She took her phone out and beamed the number to G-Dogg, who checked the display on his phone, then beamed her his number before snapping it closed.

"Frosty," he said. "I'll call you when things start happening. If something comes up, give me a buzz."

"Okay," Kellan said.

"Sure you don't want one for the road?" G-Dogg asked. "I'm buyin'."

Kellan shook her head. "No, thanks, I should get going."

"Later, then," the ork said and drove off, turning the corner around the side of the club.

Kellan waited until he was out of sight before going over to the public comm terminal and slotting her credstick, keying in a request for a cab. She hoped that the Grid-Cabs ran this late at night, but she hadn't wanted to ask G-Dogg about it and thus admit that she didn't have transportation of her own. That was something she was going to have to take care of, maybe when she got the cred from this job.

The cab showed up in short order and Kellan climbed in, slotting her stick into the port and keying in the address she needed. It highlighted the destination on a map displayed on the scratched and battered flatscreen, and she accepted the route as correct. By the time she was halfway there, it had started to rain again, a steady drumming on the roof and windows of the cab, painting the city streets in streaks of distorted streetlights and neon signs.

"Thank you for choosing Grid-Cab," the cab's voice chirped cheerfully as it pulled up to the destination. Kellan quickly pulled her stick from the slot and climbed out, hugging her jacket close against the chill rain. She dashed over to the skeletal framework of steel and ferrocrete that loomed overhead, dark against the cloudy sky.

The flickering neolux sign running up the side of the building simply said, SLEEP. From the outside, it looked something like a parking garage, which it was, in a way. Kellan walked up to the small booth that was protected by heavy, bulletproof plastic windows, slotting her credstick into the port. The attendant barely looked up from the tiny flatscreen on the counter that was showing a Matrix porn channel, waving her in with a distracted gesture. She climbed the metal-framework stairs to the third floor, her boots clanging on the catwalk. Stacked up in rows on either side were metallic cylinders about a meter wide and nearly three meters long. Their shapes had given places like this the name "coffin hotels," and in fact there was only slightly more space in one of the modules than in a typical casket.

Kellan stopped at number 314 and slotted her credstick into the port. There was a beep and the hatch of the module popped open. Kellan crawled inside, too tired to bother pulling off any of her clothes. She just keyed the controls to close the hatch behind her. It cut off most of the sound of the rain and the traffic from the street outside, and she stretched out on the temperform padding covering the floor. The only light inside the pod came from the phosphorescent glow-strips along the side; Kellan had thrown a black T-shirt over the small flatscreen that constantly advertised cheap sim-porn and other pay-per-view "entertainment" like the drek the attendant was watching.

Her brain was buzzing with everything that had happened that night, and she wondered how she would get to sleep. Not only had she managed to hook up with some work in Seattle on her second night in the metroplex, but an old-time shadowrunner told her that she was a fraggin' mage and was willing to teach her about using magic! Kellan daydreamed about what she could do once Lothan taught her how to control her magic. Like G-Dogg said, spell-slingers—good ones, at least—were always in demand in the shadows. If she learned from Lothan, she could really hit the big time. No more scrounging and scraping together enough cred to make ends meet.

"The big time . . ." Kellan murmured to herself, and she drifted off to sleep.

5

The insistent buzzing of Kellan's phone prodded her from sleep and she fumbled in the dimness of the coffin to find it.

"Mmm, 'lo?" she mumbled into it, and was greeted by the cheerful bass voice of G-Dogg in return.

"Hoi, Kellan," he said.

"Wha—what time is it?" she rolled over and pulled the shirt off the coffin's flatscreen so she could see the time display in the lower right corner at about the same time G-Dogg answered.

"It's time for biz," he said. The clock told Kellan it was 12:22 P.M. "I'm supposed to get everyone together for a meet tonight at Lothan's. I was heading out to talk to people and figured I'd see if you wanted to come with. Give you a chance to meet some people one-on-one rather than as a group. If you're not busy, that is."

Feeling more awake, Kellan decided it was a good idea. She much preferred to meet any potential teammates with G-Dogg to introduce her, rather than just being another face in the crowd at Lothan's. She sat up, careful not to bang her head against the top of the coffin.

"Yeah, that sounds wizard," she said with as much enthusiasm as she could muster.

"I'll drive," G-Dogg offered. "Where do you want me to pick you up?"

Kellan gave G-Dogg the address of a nearby Stuffer Shack. He said he knew where to find it and would see her there shortly. When he hung up, she put her phone away and gathered her gear. Everything Kellan owned was stowed in a synthleather shoulder bag tucked into the far end of the coffin, or in the pockets of her jacket. She had already realized it wasn't smart to leave anything at the coffin hotel, even though she had risked it last night. They were only supposed to allow customers inside the building, but she didn't like to trust the place's lackadaisical security with her meager possessions.

I must look like drek, Kellan thought, running her fingers through her hair in an effort to tame it, finally deciding to wear a baseball cap to keep it under control. She hadn't showered since leaving Kansas City (no way would she use the communal facilities at the coffin hotel), and she had run out of clean clothes, so she was starting to stink. Hopefully, nobody G-Dogg was going to introduce her to would care. From what she'd seen at the meeting at Ebey's Bar, her hygiene was the least of the things other people would be thinking about.

A short while later, G-Dogg's Argent pulled into the tiny parking lot of the Stuffer Shack nearest the hotel, and Kellan threw out the wrapper and last couple of bites of the Nukit breakfast burrito she was eating and climbed in, wiping her mouth on the back of her sleeve.

"Ready to get down to it?" the ork asked her. Unlike Kellan, he was dressed in different clothes than the previous night, though still the same style. Kellan noted that the vest G-Dogg was wearing today contained a thick layer of ballistic cloth beneath the outer layer of synthleather.

"All set," she told him and the ork pulled the Argent smoothly out into traffic.

"Okay," G-Dogg said, adopting a tone that was all business. "Lothan chose the people he wants on the team and asked me to find out if they're interested. It'll give you the chance to meet some of the players in this town. Chances are you're going to hear about most of them sooner or later, and probably work with most of them eventually. That's the way biz works in Seattle."

"Everybody works with everybody?" Kellan asked. "So Lothan doesn't have a regular team?" Back in Kansas City, Kellan had worked with the same group of runners from job to job. Of course, there were a lot fewer shadowrunners in Kansas City than there were in Seattle, she figured.

"Well, not everybody works that way. But like I said, Lothan's not exactly a people person. He doesn't like teams. He'd rather pick his players to suit the job and not get attached. If you ask me," the ork continued, "it's a smart way to work. Regular teams are okay, but it's good when you can put together whatever sort of team you need to do the job. It's how a lot of people work around here, so you'll get used to it."

G-Dogg headed north again, picking up 405. This time, rather than heading across Lake Washington toward Council Island, he took an exit off the highway into the Bellevue district of the metroplex instead.

"Nice area," Kellan said, looking impressed by the condoplexes, many of them surrounded by private security perimeters prominently displaying the logos of security companies like Lone Star, Knight Errant and Wolverine, proclaiming to the world that the residents were better protected because they had the nuyen to hire their own private police forces. "Where we headed?" she asked.

"You'll see," he said. "This job involves moving the goods and doing it quick, so the first guy we want to talk to is our wheelman."

The ork pulled into the lot of what looked like a renovated gas station. There were three vehicle bays next to a small office with windows of tinted glass covered with blinds on the inside. Above the garage and office was a second floor, its windows likewise covered. There were no fuel pumps, but the pavement outside was covered with grease spots and the occasional skid mark. G-Dogg parked the Argent at the side of the building. He waited until Kellan climbed out before closing his door and keying the security system.

The ork walked directly to the door closest to the first vehicle bay, where he stood, waiting. Kellan forced herself to wait patiently rather than ask G-Dogg what he was expecting. A few moments later, G-Dogg looked up, and Kellan followed his gaze to see something hanging on the wall just over the door. It looked like a metallic spider, about the size of the ork's fist, its round, silvery body supported on a set of spindly metallic legs. A single red "eye" glowed off-center in the front, and the ork gave it a tusky grin. The spider turned suddenly and scuttled up the wall, then there was a buzz and the door unlocked. G-Dogg grabbed it and pulled it all the way open, motioning for Kellan to enter.

Inside the garage was dim compared to outside. As her eyes adjusted, Kellan saw the sleek lines of cars in the vehicle bays. All around them were arrayed rolling cabinets of tools, wall racks of parts and supplies, and a profusion of metallic and cast-ceramic junk of all shapes and sizes. The car in the bay at the far end of the building was raised up on a hydraulic lift and an electric-blue glow flickered beneath it.

G-Dogg wove his way around the other cars toward the last bay and Kellan followed. Under the raised car was a multiarmed contraption wielding various tools and grippers, currently holding part of the car's chassis in place as it precisely spot-welded it. Off to the side sat a stocky figure. He was a dwarf, barely a meter and a quarter tall by Kellan's estimate. His eyes were closed as if in silent meditation, hands resting in his lap. He wore heavy work boots and a pair of dark blue coveralls stained with grease and marked with small burnt patches. His hair and beard were brown and long, braided with metallic beads and clasps, but what immediately drew Kellan's attention was the thin fiber-optic cable snaking out from the chrome-lipped jack behind his right ear. It extended behind his arm and across the floor to the welding rig under the car.

The rig made one more weld, and then its arms gracefully folded like the petals of some strange flower, dropping the drone into a resting pose. The dwarf in the chair opened his eyes and turned toward his visitors. His irises were shot through with silver circuitry that gleamed in the dim light. *Cyber-eyes*, Kellan thought.

"G-Dogg," he said in a neutral tone.

"Hey, Max, 'sup?"

"Same ol'," the dwarf replied, reaching behind his ear to pull the plug from his jack with an audible click. He stood up and tugged the cable. It started to wind smoothly into the housing of the tool rig. "Just doing some touch-up work," he said.

"Looks good," G-Dogg said, glancing over the car.

"Thanks."

"Max, this is Kellan Colt. Kellan, this is Silver Max, one of the best riggers you're ever likely to meet." The dwarf seemed to take the compliment as his due.

"Hey," Kellan said, extending a hand. Max shook it with a firm grip.

"You putting something together, G-Dogg?" he asked, turning toward the ork.

"Not me—Lothan," he said. "We need a driver, probably some overwatch, too." The dwarf raised one shaggy eyebrow.

"What would I be driving and what's the cut?"

"A cargo hauler and it's 5K on delivery."

"Combat?" the dwarf asked.

"Not much if we do it right."

"When?"

"Meeting tonight at Lothan's. Things will probably go down in a couple days."

The dwarf went over to the hydraulic lift and started inspecting the welds from underneath.

"Okay," he said curtly. "I'm in."

"Wizard," G-Dogg said. "Meet at Lothan's tonight, 2000 hours."

"I'll be there," the dwarf replied without looking away from his work. G-Dogg headed for the door and Kellan followed close behind. As they left, Silver Max picked up a wrench and began adjusting something on the undercarriage of the car.

"Okay," G-Dogg said outside the garage. "Now let's see if the intel I picked up on our next guy is good."

"Where's he?" Kellan asked as they got into the car.

"Redmond," the ork said.

They headed northeast. The neighboring area of Redmond couldn't have been more different from Bellevue if someone had planned it that way. The corporate condoplexes and gated communities gave way to streets lined with largely abandoned buildings and the occasional corporate complex surrounded by a high fence topped with razor wire. The warning signs indicated the fences were electrified and patrolled by paranormal guard animals, mostly barghests, hellhounds and cockatrices.

"Redmond used to be pretty high-class," G-Dogg said as Kellan looked over the burnt-out storefronts, broken windows covered with sheets of construction plastic and plywood with layers of gang graffiti scrawled over them. "Back around the turn of the century there was a lot of computer biz around here—baby 'net corps and drek like that. 'Course this was before the Matrix. When the Computer Crash of 2029 hit, it took the computer corps down with it. Most of them went out of business overnight and a lot of others pulled out of the area. With all the damage done by the Ghost Dance War and the other drek the metroplex was going through, well, nobody really cared about trying to fix things. So refugees and metahumans and people with nowhere else to go moved in and squatted. Now Lone Star won't come into the Barrens with anything less than an APC and full riot gear."

They passed what looked like a kind of Stuffer Shack, set up in an old gas station, the pumps long since boxed and the skeleton of the place's old sign looming overhead. Kellan saw a few girls—human and ork—working the nearby street corner, listlessly showing off their wares for any cars that cruised past.

"They call this part Touristville," G-Dogg commented in response to the surroundings. "It's right on the border with Bellevue, and some of the suits and straight citizens like to come slumming when they're looking for a little of that 'Barrens edge' to have some not-so-legal fun. It's not too bad right here, since the Star comes down hard when the locals hassle an uptown SINner. Places further east like Glow City and the Rat's Nest, the mutants and squatters there would gladly knife you for a pair of shoes, or just to make fresh meat for the ghouls."

Kellan shuddered involuntarily, though she tried to hide it. She'd heard stories about ghouls, twisted metahumans that made orks and trolls look handsome by comparison. Once they'd been human, but now they were barely intelligent creatures that fed on human (and metahuman) flesh. Bands of them lived in places like the Barrens, where they fed on corpses and occasionally hunted fresh meat among the squatters and street people. Kellan had never seen a ghoul, and wasn't particularly eager to ever see one. A lot of local municipalities offered a bounty on ghouls, considering them a threat to public safety. She had known a guy in Kansas City who made some cred on the side as a ghoul hunter, until one night when he went looking for some ghouls and he didn't come back.

Absorbed by her thoughts, Kellan barely noticed

when G-Dogg slowed the car and pulled into a lot next to a building with a scarred brick front. The lot was half exposed dirt and half cracked asphalt, enclosed by a thick chain strung from metal posts embedded in concrete. There were a number of cars and motorcycles already parked there, most of them considerably older and more beaten up than the ork's Argent. G-Dogg hit the security system as soon as they were out of the car, and led Kellan around to the front of the building.

Metal letters mounted on the crumbling brick wall read CRUSHER 495, and the few windows at the front of the building were tinted, so you couldn't see inside. G-Dogg glanced at Kellan as they approached the door.

"Just follow my lead, okay?" he said. Kellan nodded as he opened the door and stepped into the gloom beyond. She followed, letting her eyes adjust to the interior illumination, dim even compared to the overcast day outside. She wondered why the majority of the places she'd been in Seattle were deliberately kept dim or shaded. Maybe it was because metahuman eyes were capable of seeing in the dark and orks, trolls and dwarves preferred less light than humans. That, or shadowrunners and other patrons preferred the illusion of privacy that the dim lighting afforded them, or some combination of both.

The Crusher turned out to be a bar, something like

Ebey's, though it was considerably bigger. The furniture was heavy and made of metal, with an industrial look to it, designed to support the massive frames of the orks and trolls who made up the greatest percentage of the clientele. The bar ran along one side, with a riveted metal top and wide, heavy stools lined up in front of it. A permanent haze of blue-gray smoke hung near the ceiling, creating haloes around the dim fluorescent lights.

G-Dogg scanned the dozen or so patrons scattered around the bar, zeroing in on one sitting alone in the back. He headed that direction with Kellan in tow. It seemed to her that most of the patrons eyed her fiercely before returning to their drinks and their conversations. She was immediately convinced that, if she had entered the bar alone, her reception would have been actively unfriendly.

So it surprised her that the man sitting in the back of the bar, slowly sipping from a tumbler filled with some dark liquor, was human. At least Kellan thought he was—it was a little difficult to tell. He was thin and wiry, with broad shoulders beneath a leather jacket bulky with armored plates. He wore a broad-brimmed hat that hid his face in shadows, but close up Kellan could see he was hollow-cheeked, with a sharp nose and chin. His face was dead white, tattooed to look like a skull, and when he picked up the glass tumbler to take a drink, Kellan saw that his hands were chromed metal and almost skeletal, moving with a faint whir of hydraulics; cyberhands without the usual covering of synthetic flesh to give them a normal appearance.

The man barely looked up as they approached, though there was no doubt that he noticed them. He offered no greeting.

"Buy you a drink, Deacon?" G-Dogg asked. That seemed to get the man's attention and he glanced up at the ork, his face expressionless, reflective eyes unreadable.

"Already got one," he said flatly in a slow drawl, returning his gaze to the other side of the bar.

G-Dogg pulled out a chair on the other side of the table with a scrape of metal on concrete. He turned it around and sat down, straddling it. Kellan took a chair at the next table, sitting sideways so the chair's back was between her and the man G-Dogg called Deacon.

"Then how about I offer you something else?" the ork asked and Deacon paused, taking another sip of his drink before responding.

"What do you have?" he said.

"Work. Lothan is putting some biz together."

"Lothan is a miserable sinner," Deacon shot back. "A devotee of the devilish arts. What kind of work does he have to offer me?"

G-Dogg grinned, showing his tusks. "Simple job: relieving a megacorp of some of their ill-gotten gains."

The Deacon's interest seemed piqued. G-Dogg leaned in a bit closer and said one quiet word.

"Ares."

The other man didn't react, his face remaining as impassive as stone. He took another sip of his drink and set the glass back down on the table before responding.

"When?" was all he asked.

"Tonight, at Lothan's, 2000 hours."

The Deacon nodded slowly.

"See you there," G-Dogg replied, standing and turning his chair back around. Kellan got up at the same time. They turned and walked away, leaving the Deacon in the shadows, nursing his drink.

Kellan waited until they were outside before she said a word.

"Who the frag was *that?*" she asked G-Dogg.

"Calls himself the Street Deacon," he replied. "Rumor has it that he worked for a megacorp once and they shafted him. You can guess which one. Anyway, it seriously messed him up. He's been working the shadows in Seattle for years now. Claims he's an agent of divine retribution or something like that. Takes on jobs that frag over the megacorps, organized crime and anything else he considers 'sinful.' He's one of the best hired guns in the plex."

"He didn't even ask you how much the job pays."

"That's because he doesn't much care," the ork said. "He's not in it for the money, although he doesn't come cheap. Thinks he's on a mission from God. Besides, he knows me and he knows Lothan, and neither one of us would try and lowball him on price. He's not somebody I want mad at me."

"Yeah, but he said that Lothan was a miserable sinner," she persisted, and G-Dogg chuckled.

"To the Street Deacon, *everyone* is a miserable sinner, kid, including him. Doesn't mean he won't work with you. Still, you might want to keep the magic stuff on the down-low when you're around him. He seems to think that anyone who slings mojo has sold their soul to the devil."

"Great."

"Don't sweat it. Like I said, doesn't mean he won't work with you. As long as he's getting paid, it's just biz. Until somebody else pays him to be on their side, of course."

Kellan paused, standing by the open car door. "Has that happened?"

G-Dogg shrugged before climbing into the car. "Sure, happens all the time. When it does, you just try to be on the winning side, or at least stay out of the way of people like the Deacon."

"And if you can't?" Kellan asked as she climbed in. G-Dogg looked her full in the face as he started the car and put it into gear.

"That's when you're on your own, kid," he replied.

6

When G-Dogg drove them back to Capitol Hill, Kellan thought they'd contacted everyone they were supposed to and were headed back to Lothan's. As it turned out, they had one more stop to make before they returned to the troll mage's house. G-Dogg found a parking space along a side street a short distance from Lothan's. He slotted his credstick into the meter, which automatically deducted the charge for parking and began counting down the time they could stay in that spot.

G-Dogg led Kellan past a few small storefronts and a coffee shop. The sidewalks were full of people going about their business and studiously ignoring each other. Some were talking on the phone, either with tiny cell phones pressed to their ears or simply talking to empty space, using subdermal implants that linked them directly into the cell network.

Kellan saw a small group of girls, probably only a couple years younger than her, checking out the trid ads for the latest Darkvine album and its associated fashion accessories in the window of a store, chattering among themselves. Kellan felt a surge of disdain for the obviously privileged daughters of well-off straight-citizen parents, but she also felt a touch of jealousy. They were the type of girls Kellan had been waiting on in restaurants and stores before she struck out on her own, kissing their perfectly sculpted butts for minimum wage. For a moment, Kellan wondered what it was like to come from a family with money, not having to wonder when and what you were going to eat next, where you were going to sleep, whether or not you'd be able to get a job to make enough cred to survive. She wondered how it would have been different if her mother had been around.

Her hand brushed against the cool jade of the amulet at her neck. Her mother. Who was she? What happened to her? When she was girl, Kellan used to imagine that her mother was somebody important, that she had left Kellan behind in order to protect her—not because she didn't care, like her aunt said. She used to hope that her mother would come back for her, though that hope diminished as the years passed with no word. Kellan's aunt swore that her mother was dead.

Now, out of the blue, she had this connection, however small, to her mother. Was she the one who sent the package? The note said, "This stuff belonged to your mother"—probably not something her mother would say, unless she didn't want Kellan to know she was alive. Kellan wanted the chance to find out, but she'd need resources and connections to do it.

Working with Lothan and G-Dogg was the first step toward the day when she made the big score and had credit to burn. For sure then, she could find out what happened to her mother. She would be the one calling the shots.

"Want to know your fortune?" a voice close to Kellan asked, and she turned to see a woman sitting behind a card table set up in front of a coffee shop. An antique-looking black shawl covered the table and a spread of tarot cards was laid out on top of the lacy silk. The woman was an elf, wearing a close-fitting T-shirt under a cloak pinned at the shoulder with a circular broach in a Celtic knot design. Her loose-fitting jeans were painted with mystical symbols and designs. Her hair was sandy colored and worn long, cascading in waves down her shoulders; and of course she was gorgeous, with intense blue eyes that seemed to look right into Kellan's soul.

"The cards know all," she said grandly, with a sweeping gesture over the table. "Just twenty nuyen for the secret insights from the elven Tree of Life."

"How's about telling *my* fortune, Liada?" G-Dogg said, and the woman smiled up at him.

"I don't give out freebies, G," she replied. In reply the ork pulled a crumpled UCAS twenty-dollar bill from his pocket and tossed it in the upturned top hat at Liada's feet.

"Okay," she shrugged. "Let's see what the cards have to say." She shuffled the deck with crisp, practiced motions before dividing them into three piles in front of her. Then she closed her eyes for a moment, letting out a slow sigh.

"Past, present and future," she said, tapping each of the stacks of cards in turn. She flipped over the top card on the first stack. It was the four of pentacles, showing masons working on a half-finished tower or castle with stained-glass windows.

"Hard work, laying the foundations for material success," the woman said. "Hustling to get things done," she glanced sidelong at G-Dogg with a slight smile, then flipped over the top card on the next stack.

It was the king of wands. "A dark man," she continued, "strong-willed, intellectual. . . ." She paused and looked up at G-Dogg again, her mouth pinched in a thin line. Then she turned over the top card on the final stack.

The princess of wands, wielding a burning torch that illuminated the darkness. "A young woman," she said, "with a passionate nature, showing the right path." She glanced up at Kellan, and then back at G-Dogg, leaning back from the table with a sigh.

"What does Lothan want?" she asked, picking up the cards and putting them back into the deck. She squared them by tapping the deck against the table before putting the cards into a small embroidered leather pouch.

"We're setting up a meeting. . . ." G-Dogg began.

"Not interested," Liada replied with a wave of her hand.

"You making that much money telling fortunes?" G-Dogg replied.

"It's not bad," she said, somewhat defensively, "but it has nothing to do with that. I just don't feel like working with the Almighty Master of the Arts Arcane." She did a deliberately bad imitation of Lothan's lofty tone, waving one hand in the air in a grand gesture.

"It's a simple job," G-Dogg said.

"It's never that simple with Lothan. You know that."

"Yeah, well, I also know that you were his first choice for magical backup on this job."

"Backup," Liada repeated. "Which means playing second fiddle to the Master. No thanks."

"Okay," G-Dogg shrugged. "I'll just tell him you weren't up for it."

The elf raised one eyebrow and glared at the smiling ork. Then she slipped the tarot deck case into the voluminous shoulder bag sitting on the ground next to her.

"When's the meeting?" she asked.

"At Lothan's, 2000 hours."

"I'll be there," she said. "I'll listen to what he has to say, but no promises. If I don't like what I hear, I'm telling Lothan where he can stick his job and I'm out of there."

"Fair enough," G-Dogg said.

"You in on this?" Liada said, turning to Kellan.

"Yeah," she replied.

"Watch out for this one," she said nodding her head toward G-Dogg, "and Lothan. The one thing they have in common is that they're both manipulative bastards." G-Dogg grinned, but didn't deny it.

"I'm Liada," she extended a hand to Kellan who shook it.

"Kellan."

"New to Seattle?" she asked.

"Yeah."

"Well, nice to meet you."

"She's Lothan's new apprentice," G-Dogg offered, which caused Liada to raise both eyebrows.

"Oh, really?" she said. "Well, my condolences. Here's hoping you survive the experience." She turned to G-Dogg, rising from behind the table. "Tell his highness that I'll be there tonight."

They still had some time before the meet after leaving Liada, so G-Dogg suggested getting something to eat. Kellan's stomach reminded her that she hadn't had anything except most of a breakfast burrito all day, so she agreed. Ensconced in a back booth at A Little Bit O' Saigon in Capitol Hill, she and the ork talked a bit.

"Why all that work just to get in touch with people?" Kellan asked. "Seems like Lothan could have handled that biz with three phone calls."

G-Dogg began ticking things off on his fingers and, for the first time, Kellan noticed that the ork had six fingers on each hand. She remembered hearing something about an extra finger being a "secondary mutation." Only a minor percentage of orks had the extra finger. It certainly was a lot less inconvenient than some other mutations that had sprung up after the Awakening.

"Well, first," he said, "Lothan doesn't like to handle stuff like that and, as you might guess, he's not all that good at it. Me, I like to talk, and I like to do my biz face-to-face.

"Second, you gotta be careful doing business over the phone. You never know who might be listening. Job like this, probably not a big deal, but there're deckers who make a living putting together random pieces of data off the Matrix, making connections and passing them on to the right people willing to pay for them. There's always a chance that somebody is going to hear when there's a run going down. You try to keep that as quiet as possible. Plus, it's easier to get a feel for what people are thinking when you're looking at them instead of talking to them on the phone."

"There a third?" Kellan asked.

"Yup. Third is I wanted you to get a chance to meet everyone and learn a little about how the biz works here in Seattle."

"Doesn't seem like Lothan is anybody's favorite guy," Kellan mused, changing the subject. She appreciated the ork's consideration, but she didn't want to dwell on the fact that she needed to be introduced around like a complete newbie.

"Lothan can have a pretty high opinion of himself," G-Dogg said, "but let me tell you, he knows the biz like nobody else. Lothan has been running the shadows longer than anybody I know. He may not be Mr. Personality, but he knows what he's doing, and that's what really counts in this business.

That's why people still work with him, even if he can be a real pain in the hoop sometimes."

"Is that why you work with him?" she asked.

"One of the reasons," G-Dogg said. "Let's just say that I owe Lothan and leave it at that, okay? He's helped me out, so I help him out."

As soon as they finished eating, they headed back to Lothan's place, where they were the first to arrive for the meeting. The old troll was all business, and wanted to wait until everyone was there before discussing the job. They assembled in Lothan's study, sitting in a rough semicircle against the backdrop of the overloaded bookshelves. Liada arrived next, followed by Silver Max and then the Street Deacon and Orion. Once everyone was in the study, Lothan settled into the wide chair in front of his desk. He turned the screen of the telecom unit on his desk to face into the room and hit a key on the control pad. A green light glowed on the display to show that it was in use.

"I believe that most of you know Jackie Ozone, by reputation, if nothing else," Lothan said, nodding toward the telecom. The screen lit up with the cartoonlike image of a girl with big eyes, a tiny, delicate mouth and long, dark hair, dressed in a flowing white gown and carrying a silvery wand. She bowed with a flourish of the wand, which trailed a sparkle of stardust behind it.

"Hello, all," came a bright voice from the tele-com's speakers.

"Now that we're all here," Lothan said. "Let's get down to business. The job is a fairly simple snatch and grab on some cargo coming into the metroplex by truck. It belongs to Ares Macrotechnology, and information from our employer indicates that there will be some modest security protecting the ship-ment."

"What's in it?" Silver Max asked.

Lothan shrugged. "The Johnson felt that was on a need-to-know basis—"

"—and we don't need to know," Max concluded, nodding for the troll to continue.

"We need to hit the truck after it gets into the metroplex, then deliver it to a location in Redmond specified by our client. Since it is coming into the plex via the East Road, our best shot is to get to the truck while it's still in Redmond, before it reaches Bellevue."

"It's headed for the Ares facility there?" Liada asked. Lothan nodded.

"Sounds simple enough," Silver Max said.

"The cut is five thousand nuyen each upon suc-cessful completion of the run," Lothan said, looking around at the runners. "Time is somewhat limited, since the shipment arrives in two days. That gives us less than forty-eight hours to confirm the details and set up the run." He looked around at the assembled runners. "Are we all in agreement on the terms?"

"Seems like you've got more muscle than you need," the Street Deacon drawled laconically, looking at G-Dogg and Orion.

"I think a little extra firepower is prudent," Lothan replied, "but you're welcome to opt out if you're feeling crowded."

The Deacon shot Lothan a thin-lipped smile that made Kellan's blood go cold. "It's your money," he said.

"Any other comments?" the troll asked. "Very well. Here are your assignments. Max, the truck should be a standard Ares cargo hauler."

"Manned?"

"Yes, but with rigger controls. So we're going to need you on-site to drive it once it's secure."

"No problem," the dwarf said. "Am I running interference before that?"

"Surveillance," Lothan said. "I want your drones to track the truck's progress to the target location we choose. I also want you to scout out the route and pinpoint the sites where we can take the truck with the minimum of witnesses and trouble." The rigger nodded, the silver baubles in his braids glinting.

"Jackie, my dear," Lothan said to the telecom. "Your job will be to cast your nets and gather all the information the Matrix has to offer about this shipment. Verify the information from our Mr. Johnson and find out what you can about the security we'll be facing."

The cute cartoon face shifted into a girlish pout. "Is that all?" she asked. "Lothan, I thought this was going to be interesting. That doesn't sound like a challenge."

"You never know until you try," the troll said, "and you are not allowed to make things any more 'interesting' than they already are, okay?"

"Spoilsport," the decker said with a spritely laugh.

"Liada," the troll continued, ignoring Jackie's persona sticking out her tongue on the monitor, "I'd like you to do astral reconnaissance of the route, just to be sure there aren't any surprises. Then I'd like to discuss the coordination of our magical offensive and defenses with you."

"All right," the elven mage said, looking vaguely bored. "So are you going on this little run with us, then?"

"Absolutely." Lothan replied in a tone that made it clear that he didn't trust any of them to handle things without his supervision.

"G-Dogg," he turned to the ork bouncer. "Is I-90 currently claimed by anyone?"

G-Dogg opened his mouth to reply, but Orion spoke up from the opposite side of the room.

"The Rusted Stilettos and the Red Hot Nukes both claim it," the elf said, "but neither of them has got much of a hold on it from what I've heard."

Lothan looked to G-Dogg for confirmation and the ork nodded. "That sounds about right to me," he said. "I think the Stilettos are probably the contenders, since Glow City is so close to the highway and nobody really wants their territory along 202."

"Yeah, but the Nukes are the ones with the bikes," the elf countered, "and they've been making their way further down the highway from Hollywood lately."

Lothan addressed G-Dogg. "I want you to find out about their recent activities," the mage told him. "See if we're likely to have any trouble with them." Then he turned to Orion. "Do you think you can find out anything from your contacts?"

"I can ask around," the elf said.

"Do so, but discreetly. And that warning goes for the rest of you, too. I don't want word of this job getting out. Even though our window is short, I don't want our target to be forewarned."

"We'll meet again tomorrow at the same time," Lothan said, "to review the plan and adjust it if necessary. Unless there are any other questions?"

"Um, yeah," Kellan said, glancing around the room. "What am I supposed to do?"

Lothan smiled indulgently. "I have something special in mind for you, Kellan," he said. "Since, as I understand it, most of your contacts in Seattle are here in this room, I have chosen a very special role for you in our little drama. You can stay here tonight, if you wish, and we'll get to work early tomorrow." Liada snorted, which Kellan did her best to ignore. She nodded.

"Okay," she told the troll.

"Don't worry, honey," Jackie Ozone's voice said from the telecom. "Lothan's not the ladies' man that he once was, though it's true what they say about a man with some experience!" Her persona rolled her large eyes and giggled girlishly. Kellan saw Lothan's bushy white brows draw together, and she would swear that the big troll blushed.

"I'd say we're done here," he said, hitting a key on the telecom pad with a blunt finger. The screen suddenly went dark. Liada and G-Dogg chuckled softly as the runners got to their feet and said their good-byes before heading for the door. Orion and the Street Deacon had nothing to say before they made their exit, although the others lingered for a moment to talk.

"So," G-Dogg asked Kellan. "You crashing here tonight?"

She glanced at Lothan a moment before responding, and the troll mage said, "I assure you, Kellan, despite Jackie's childish jibes, you have nothing to fear from me. There's a guest room where you can stay, and the door locks, if it makes you feel any better."

"Guess so," she said turning back to G-Dogg. The ork nodded and punched her gently in the arm before he left.

As the other runners showed themselves out, Kellan's phone rang.

" 'Lo?" she said, and the spritely voice of Jackie Ozone greeted her.

"Lothan's okay," the decker said, "but watch your back anyway."

"Thanks," Kellan said in as neutral a tone as possible. "I will."

"Here's a number where you can contact me." Kellan's phone beeped as it received the data. "Give me a buzz if you need anything. Welcome to Seattle," Jackie said with a laugh. "Be seeing you." Then the decker hung up. As she closed her phone and put it away, Kellan realized that she hadn't asked Jackie how she'd gotten her number.

7

Although Lothan's guest room wasn't lavish, it was still the nicest place Kellan had slept in a long time—for sure since she had been out on her own. There was no comparison to the coffin hotel she had been crashing at since she arrived in Seattle. She didn't miss the cramped quarters or the thin temperform padding one bit, and slept like a stone, despite the unusual surroundings and Jackie Ozone's somewhat ominous warning to watch herself around Lothan.

Nothing and no one disturbed her sleep and Kellan awoke feeling truly refreshed. She sat up in bed and stretched luxuriously, feeling her joints pop, and exhaled a deep breath.

"Oh, good, you're up!" a voice said. Kellan yelped

and whipped her head around to find the source of the voice.

Hovering above the headboard was a tiny figure, less than half a meter tall. It was humanoid, with a broad head that consisted mostly of a prominent nose and large, pointed ears. It had somewhat spindly arms and legs but large hands and feet. Especially striking were the batlike wings, the forked tail and the fact that the creature was translucent; Kellan could see the wall on the other side of it.

"Who . . . what are you?" she asked, the blankets pulled up to her chin. The little creature bowed at the waist (such as it was) and waved an arm.

"Nicodemus, I am," it said in its high-pitched voice. "The master set me to wait and watch for you to awaken, he did. 'Tell her when she wakes,' he said."

"Tell me what?"

Nicodemus seemed taken aback by that question and paused for a moment. His eyes rolled up and his brow furrowed in concentration as he rubbed his chin.

"Hmmm," he mused.

"Tell me what?" Kellan repeated, and the little imp seemed to snap out of his reverie.

"Said to tell you that you should wash and eat before you work today," he replied. "Said to show you where everything is, and that he is not to be disturbed until he is ready. Come.'' The spirit zipped closer to Kellan and waved with one hand. ''Come, I will show you.''

Kellan gathered up her clothing and cautiously followed the floating figure out of the room. Nicodemus led her to a bathroom, where Kellan shooed the imp away and enjoyed her second great pleasure of the last twelve hours: a long, hot shower. About halfway through, it occurred to her that this bathroom must be exclusively for guests: the facilities weren't nearly large enough for a troll; Lothan would have only barely fit into the room.

She was almost finished washing her hair when the imp passed through the frosted glass door of the shower like a ghost.

''Do you want to eat now?'' Nicodemus asked cheerfully. Kellan yelled and threw the soap at him, chasing him out of the shower. She found the spirit hovering outside the bathroom when she'd dried off and dressed. She wished she'd had the chance to clean her clothes, but it appeared that would have to wait. Nicodemus' enthusiasm seemed undiminished by her outburst in the shower, and he led her to the kitchen, where Kellan found a plentiful supply of convenience food that even her limited cooking skills could handle. She popped a breakfast entree into the microwave and soon was dining on a meal that contained less soy than any meal she'd had in a while. Lothan clearly did all right for himself in the biz.

Nicodemus hovered nearby, silently watching Kellan go about her business. She realized that he was probably guarding her as much as helping her, assigned to keep an eye on Lothan's guest and make sure that she didn't cause Lothan any headaches. Lothan was a wily old troll, that was for sure.

If Lothan can teach me how to do stuff like that, she thought, glancing at Nicodemus, *then G-Dogg is right: I can write my own ticket in this biz.*

It bothered her, though, that everyone G-Dogg had introduced her to yesterday seemed wary of Lothan, if not outright contemptuous. They were willing to work with him, but they didn't seem to like him very much. Even G-Dogg, who stood up for Lothan, didn't seem like the troll's best friend. Then there was Jackie Ozone's warning. What did she mean about Kellan "watching her back" around Lothan? Kellan was experienced and mature enough to understand that you didn't have to like everyone you worked with, but she was a little worried about the apparently universal attitude toward Lothan.

"So, feeling fortified for the day?"

Kellan started at the sound of Lothan's voice, and turned to see the old troll looming in the doorway of the kitchen. She choked down the food she was chewing and pushed her plate away.

"Yeah, all set," she said quickly.

"Nicodemus said that you were awake. I had begun to think that you were going to sleep the day away, but I'm sure you needed the rest."

"Um, thanks," Kellan said. "What time is it, anyway?"

"A little after ten," Lothan replied. "Still plenty of time to begin your training. We shouldn't be hearing from the others until this evening. Are you ready?" he asked.

"I guess so."

"Excellent. Then why don't you join me in my study and we'll get started. Nicodemus?" he said to the hovering spirit.

"Yes, master?"

"I won't be needing you any further for now. You are dismissed."

"Yes, master." Nicodemus bowed, then there was a tiny puff of wispy red smoke and the little imp vanished. Lothan turned and left the room without another word.

Kellan cleared away the remains of her breakfast and retraced her steps to Lothan's study. The house was considerably brighter and less spooky during the daytime, though Kellan noticed that Lothan had the heavy drapes drawn over the windows even during the day.

When she entered the study, Lothan gestured to an empty chair set opposite his own.

"Have a seat," the troll invited.

On the low table between the two chairs were laid out a number of familiar objects: several candles in tarnished brass holders, scraps of paper, a few rough-faceted crystals and a datapad. She had no idea how Lothan would use them in her lesson. Once Kellan sat down, the mage settled back into his own massive chair with a quiet sigh.

"So," he said. "Tell me, what is magic?"

"Magic?" Kellan repeated. "It's, you know, spells and stuff." She waved her hand vaguely in the air. "The ability to make things happen." Lothan nodded encouragingly.

"Not bad," he said, "albeit quaintly phrased. Magic," he began, holding up an index finger for emphasis, "is defined as the art and science of causing change with the will." He opened his upheld hand with a flourish and in his palm blossomed the image of a beautiful nude woman with elfin features and tiny gossamer wings on her back. She was little more than ten centimeters tall, and spun and danced a complex ballet in the hollow of the troll's palm. Kellan gaped at how realistic she looked.

Then Lothan turned his hand over and dismissed the image with a wave. It dissipated in a shower of faerie dust and was gone.

"A parlor trick," the troll said with a degree of false modesty. "Magic can be used for far more useful and interesting things."

"Such as?" Kellan asked dryly. It was clear that Lothan intended to begin at the very beginning. If she were to be honest with herself, however, she had to admit that was a good thing, since she knew very little about what magic was and how it worked.

"Theoretically, magic can do virtually anything," Lothan said, ignoring her tone and settling back in his chair again. "But practically, it's a bit more limited than that. Magic is the ability to perceive and shape certain forces, called mana, toward certain ends. It's dependent upon the knowledge and the will of the magician using it. The more you know about how to shape magical forces and the stronger your will to direct them, the more you can accomplish. For example, the feat of magic that G-Dogg described you performing—setting fire to that ganger—is no easy trick."

"But I don't even know how I did that."

"Precisely," Lothan replied. "You have talent, but it's raw, untrained and undisciplined. It responds solely to your emotions and your subconscious desires, and even then only in times of the direst need. It's how many with the Talent discover their potential—when something forces it to the surface and they invoke the power for the first time. Tell me, how did you feel immediately after the incident?"

"Really tired," Kellan said. "Totally wiped. In fact, I passed out."

"Quite right. That is because using magic takes its toll on body, mind and spirit. Channeling magical energy takes effort, just the same as doing something with your hands or other muscles. Using too much magic can be draining, but, like strengthening any other muscle, you can build up your magical power. A simple spell like the one I just showed you is practically no effort at all for me, but an elemental spell like the one you used in that alley would be an effort for most spellcasters, though less draining than it was for you. It would be even easier for someone with my skills."

"Now then," Lothan said, setting his hands on his knees and leaning forward a bit. "We've established what magic is. Let's consider a bit more how it happens, shall we?" When Kellan nodded her agreement, he continued. "As I said, magic involves a certain kind of energy, called mana. Mana, the source of magical power, is an invisible force that's present all around us." He gestured expansively with his arms for emphasis. "It's like the air we breathe, or perhaps like the constant stream of radio and broadcast signals all around us. Magicians—those with the Talent—are like antennas, able to tune in to the right frequencies and channel mana."

"Can you run out of energy?" Kellan asked.

"Not really. It's far more likely that a magician will exhaust his ability to channel mana before ever exhausting the source of the energy itself, though there are some cases where mana can be aspected toward a particular . . . But I digress," the troll said, wagging a finger at Kellan.

"Now where was I . . . ? Ah, yes. Magicians shape mana in a few specific ways. First is to cause effects in the physical world, ranging from creating glamours and illusions like the one I showed you to hurling fire and lightning, levitating objects, or even transforming physical structure. This is the art of sorcery, and it is the primary art of magic. Second, magicians channel mana to open gateways to the metaplanes to summon and bind various sorts of spirits to do their bidding. This is the art of conjuring."

"Is that how you summoned Nicodemus?"

"Yes, a minor feat of conjury," Lothan said with a nod. "Watcher spirits like Nicodemus are useful for some minor tasks, but they can't be entrusted with too much. Their capacities are rather limited. There are far more powerful spirits, but they are more dangerous to summon and more difficult to control. We'll discuss conjuring further at some point, but for now it's best to focus on the basics." Kellan nodded and allowed Lothan to continue.

"Finally," the troll said, "magicians invest mana into physical objects, giving those objects magical properties and making them useful tools in performing magic. This is the art of enchanting, which produces things like your amulet," gesturing toward Kellan's necklace, "and this."

Lothan reached over and picked up a heavy staff from where it rested next to his desk. It was made of wood, gnarled and carved with mystical symbols and writing. It was topped with a reddish crystal that gleamed in the sunlight that filtered through the heavy curtains. It was decorated with bands of copper and bronze.

"The Staff of Candor-Brie," Lothan intoned. "One of the more useful trinkets I've acquired over the years."

Kellan could almost feel the magic radiating from the massive staff, like a wave of static electricity tingling across her skin.

"What does it do?" she asked.

"It's not what a particular focus does that is important, but what it allows *you* to do. A focus is just that: a tool for focusing the magical abilities and powers of its wielder. It's of no use to someone without the Talent, and the more capable the wielder, the more effective the focus can be." He carefully replaced the staff, then rubbed his hands briskly. "Enough theory for the moment. Let's try something a bit more practical."

Lothan picked up a thick candle from the table

between them, checking the fit of the bottom of the taper in the old brass candleholder before setting it in the middle of the table.

"Now then, since you've already demonstrated an affinity for setting things on fire," the mage said with a smile, "let's try an experiment." He gestured toward the fresh wick of the candle. "Light this candle."

"How?" Kellan asked, looking from the taper to the troll and back.

"Well, first," Lothan said, "clear your mind. Don't think about *how* it's done. Take a deep breath. That's it. Now I want to you focus on the wick of the candle. Allow your attention to rest on it, but don't allow your focus to drift. It's critical when doing magic to be able to see the subject of your spell," he continued in a low, soothing tone of voice. "The image of your subject is a key part of the spell.

"Now I want you to concentrate on the image of fire. Feel the heat rushing through your limbs. Hear the roar and crackle of it. Feel it burning inside of you, building up. Feel the idea, the *essence* of fire. Take hold of it. Direct it toward the wick of the candle. Take hold of the fire within you, make it yours, and direct it."

The candle remained unlit. "It's not working," Kellan said.

"Patience, patience," Lothan replied. "Concentrate.

I want you to remember your encounter in the alley, when you saw G-Dogg fighting. Remember how you felt when the ork grabbed you. Remember when you were fighting for your life."

Kellan recalled Horse's sneering face, his rough voice threatening violence, the smell of him looming over her. A reddish haze surrounded the edges of her vision and her skin felt hot.

"Yes," Lothan said softly. "Take the fire, Kellan. It is yours. Direct it at the candle."

There was a dull roaring in Kellan's ears. Then she raised one hand and pointed at the candle, thrusting her finger forward. The building energy seemed to pour out of her like water from a hose and the candle suddenly burst into flames. Not just a tiny flame, but a gout of fire that shot up toward the ceiling. The candle instantly melted and Lothan cursed, waving his hands in the air.

Kellan slumped in the chair and the flames went out as suddenly as they'd appeared. A puddle of molten wax slowly spread across the table, but otherwise the study was no worse the wear for the unexpected fire. Kellan felt tired, but not as drained as she had felt in the alley.

"I'm sorry," she told Lothan, but the troll mage shook his head.

"It's all right, your spell was just a bit more . . . vigorous than I expected," he said. "I'll just have to take that into account next time. Still, it was an excellent first step."

"It was?" Kellan replied.

"Absolutely. Many fledgling magicians take weeks or months before they are able to cast their first spell. You seem to have picked up this one almost instinctively. This effect is an elemental manipulation commonly called a flamethrower."

"So I cast a spell? That's all there is to it?" Kellan asked. "What about the magic words and stuff?" she gestured vaguely with one hand, making a mystical-looking pass through the air.

Lothan chuckled. "I'll let you in on yet another of the secrets of wizardry," he said, leaning in toward Kellan. "The truth is that all the chants, the magic words, the grand gestures—they're just window dressing. Useful, to be sure, because they help you to focus your mind and your will on what it is you're doing—and that can be vital when you need to cast the right spell in a hurry—but it's not strictly necessary. The pointing, for example," he nodded at the melted candle on the table, "that was a nice touch, and it probably helped you direct the spell, but you could have accomplished the same thing without it."

Just then, a glowing point of light passed through the door of the study. It was like the light that led Kellan and G-Dogg through the house the previous night—perhaps the same one. Kellan couldn't tell, though now she could guess that it was some kind of watcher spirit, similar to Nicodemus. It floated over to Lothan and hovered by the troll's horns for a moment. He cocked his head and seemed to be listening to something Kellan couldn't hear. Then he waved his hand in a gesture of dismissal, and the light sped out of the room as he turned back to Kellan.

"Let's take a short break, shall we? Allow you some time to catch your breath and rest a bit after your exertion. Other business calls: we have a visitor."

8

"Liada, do come in," Lothan said. The elven woman stepped into the study, adjusting the bulky bag she wore over her shoulder and glancing briefly at Kellan.

"I astrally scouted out the route," she told Lothan with no preamble. "I don't think we'll have any problems with contamination from Glow City or any of the other hot spots in the Barrens, though it's not exactly the cleanest astral environment."

"Good, good," Lothan said, getting to his feet. He picked up a datapad from his desk and tapped the keys a couple times before handing it across the table to Kellan.

"Kellan, here are some introductory texts I'd like

you to review. Please excuse us while we talk business, won't you?"

Kellan looked at the proferred datapad before taking it from Lothan's hand and glancing over at Liada.
The elf's face was as unreadable as Lothan's.

"Yeah, sure," she said flatly, getting up from her
chair and heading for the door. Liada closed it behind her and she could hear the two magicians talking in low voices. Kellan clutched the datapad and
stalked down the hall to the kitchen. She almost
slammed it onto the big, heavy table in the middle
of the room.

Fraggit! Just when she was starting to think that
Lothan and the others were taking her seriously, he
treats her like a child, giving her a toy to play with
and sending her off into a corner while the grown-
ups talk! She thought that she was supposed to be a
member of the team. Why did Lothan want her out
of the way?

Was Lothan up to something, trying to keep her
in the dark while he set her up? Was Liada's warning
a game of misdirection, to get Kellan to mistrust Lothan? Were she and Lothan in on it together?

Kellan took a deep breath. These were crazy
thoughts. After all, Lothan and the others hardly
knew her, right? They weren't going to trust her
overnight. They were professional shadowrunners.

They were going to hedge their bets, play things safe, until they knew that Kellan was okay. So she would just have to prove to them that she was, that she could handle anything they had to throw at her.

Kellan dropped into a chair and picked up the datapad. It displayed a text entitled "The Essentials of Modern Thaumaturgical Theory" by Miles Swinburne, Th.D. She looked at the page display and saw that Lothan's idea of a "basic text" was nearly two hundred pages long.

Geez, isn't there a vid-version of this?

"I can handle it," she muttered to herself. "Whatever it takes," and she settled back to start reading.

The document was just as dry and dull as Kellan had feared, but it still managed to be interesting. It elaborated on some of the concepts Lothan had been talking about, describing the existence of the astral plane, the magical energy called mana and how magicians used both to do magic. A few times Kellan had to ask the datapad's dictionary to define a term, but she was pretty confident that she understood most of it. There was certainly a lot of information to absorb. What little she'd seen of magic seemed so simple that it was hard to accept that it was really so complicated. Even the stuff Lothan did; he seemed to just wave his hands, say a few words and things happened. Apparently, a lot of explanations, diagrams and theories went into explaining that process.

A faint creak of the floorboards in the hall caught Kellan's attention. She looked up from her reading as Liada strolled into the kitchen.

"How's it going?" the elf asked her, nodding toward the datapad.

Kellan sighed. "Okay. This book is really long."

Liada laughed. "That isn't the half of it," she said. "There are entire libraries full of books on magic and magic theory. Just look at all the dead trees Lothan has lining the walls of his study."

Kellan thought about having to read all of those books and shuddered. "How do you remember it all?" she asked.

"You don't really need to," Liada said, going over to the counter and pouring herself a cup of soykaf from the dispenser. "Once you know the basics, it's mostly just variations on a theme. The really complex stuff is only used for rituals, and even old-timers like Lothan crack the books then to make sure they're getting it right." She brought the steaming cup over to the table and sat down across from Kellan, taking a sip and making a face at the bitter taste.

"Of course," she continued, "Lothan will make everything seem at least ten times more complicated and mystical than it needs to be, and he'll probably have you reading drek that you'll never really use. . . ." She reached over and picked up the datapad, turning it around to read the display.

"Swinburne?" she said, with a raised eyebrow. "See, that's the kind of thing I'm talking about. Swinburne's stuff is old news, written more than thirty years ago, but mages like Lothan still consider it a Classical Foundation of Modern Hermetics." She managed to vocally capitalize the last four words. "I'm surprised he didn't start you off reading Waite, Crowley and Carroll, while he was at it." Kellan didn't recognize the names, but it was clear Liada didn't hold them in especially high regard.

"So what should I be reading?" Kellan asked.

"If you ask me, you should be doing something other than just reading," Liada replied, taking another sip of her coffee substitute. "Reading is all well and good, and there are some perfectly good *modern* grimoires and texts available on the Matrix, but there's no substitute for practice."

"We did some of that," Kellan said, a bit sheepishly. "I almost set the place on fire."

Liada laughed again. "I wish I could have seen Lothan's face when that happened."

"Where *is* Lothan?" Kellan asked, glancing toward the hall.

"Meditating," Liada replied. "Checking up on me is more like it. He wants to make absolutely certain that everything is ready."

"More of that 'astral scouting' you were talking about?"

"Yeah, although I'm better at that sort of thing than Lothan, if you ask me," Liada said with a smile. "But if he wants to double-check, that's his business."

"What's it like? The astral plane, I mean. Part of what I read today talked about that."

Liada thought for a moment. "How do you explain what color is like to someone who's been blind all their life?" she said. "No offense," she added, seeing the expression on Kellan's face. "But you said you didn't have any experience with it. That's the hard part about the astral plane. It's a place that isn't really a place, because it's right next door to the physical world, in a way. You see it with a kind of psychic sixth sense, by doing what we call assensing. It lets you sense emotions, mana flows, magical impressions, things like that. Most people see them as colored auras of light, though some perceive them as sounds, or smells, or just strong feelings. It's tough to describe. That's what I mean about experiencing it for yourself. But once you do, there's no greater sense of freedom in the world."

"Sounds wiz," Kellan said.

"Yeah, it is. But don't fool yourself—the astral plane can be dangerous, too. Spirits live there, and some of them aren't too friendly. In fact, some of them are downright nasty."

Liada studied Kellan for a moment like she was

trying to assess something about her, and Kellan wondered if the elf was seeing or "assensing" her as she'd said, using that special kind of magical sight.

"I'm kind of surprised you haven't had any experience with the astral," Liada continued. "Some kind of spontaneous assensing or astral projection is pretty common with newly Awakened magicians."

Kellan shook her head. "The only real magical experience I've had was when I set this troll ganger on fire, and the stuff that Lothan has been trying to teach me."

"Interesting. Is Lothan sure that you're a mage?"

"Well, he said that I definitely have the Talent," Kellan said.

"Yes, but is he sure that you're a mage and not a shaman?"

Kellan was puzzled. "What's the difference?"

"Typical," Liada said with a sad shake of her head. "I should have expected that kind of attitude from Lothan." When Kellan continued to give her a quizzical look, she went on. "Magicians are people with the Talent for tapping into and using mana to do magic, but there are different traditions of magic, magicians who do magic in different ways. Mages are magicians who follow the hermetic tradition, like Lothan and like me, but we're not the only kind of magicians. Far from it, in fact."

"Right," Kellan said, "they have shamans in the

Native American Nations, like the ones that led the Ghost Dance."

Liada chuckled. "They don't have many shamans like *that* anymore," she said. "But, yeah, the NAN has a lot of shamans, although shamans aren't just a Native American thing. They're all over the place."

"So what's the difference between shamans and mages?" Kellan asked.

"Shamans have the guidance of spirits they call totems. They're these powerful spirits that come to the shamans in visions and dreams and tell them how to do magic. They usually show up as different kinds of animals. Through their totems, shamans tap into the power of the natural world. They can contact the spirits of nature and ask them to do things. Have you ever had any dreams where an animal was talking to you, maybe trying to tell you something or teach you a song or special name?"

Kellan thought for a moment and then shook her head. "I don't think so," she replied. "At least, I don't remember anything like that. I don't usually remember my dreams."

"You may now that you've Awakened," Liada said, taking another sip of her soykaf. "Doesn't sound to me like you've been called by a totem, but you never know. You should keep track of your dreams and see if they have anything to tell you. Try keeping a dream journal, writing down what you remember as soon as you wake up. There are a lot of symbols and messages in our dreams."

"How will I know if I'm supposed to be a shaman?" she asked.

"Oh, you'll know, believe me," she said. "The totems have their own way of revealing things, and when they want you to know something, they're not subtle."

"If you're not a shaman," Kellan wondered, "then how come you know so much about them?"

"Some of my best friends are shamans," Liada said, "and, unlike His Majesty," she nodded her head toward Lothan's study, "I think there's something to be gained from studying other traditions of magic and knowing how other people do things." Kellan thought that made sense.

Just then, the glowing light-sprite zipped into the room to hover above the table, bobbing gently toward Liada, then toward the door.

"Oops," she said. "Looks like he's done. Better go see what he has to say." She stood up from the table, leaving the mug where it sat. "Talk to you later, Kellan."

"Yeah. And thanks," Kellan told the elf.

"No problem," she replied. "We'll talk again sometime, okay?"

"I'd like that," Kellan said. She went back to her reading with a new appreciation for the material. She would have to ask Lothan about shamanism and those different traditions of magic Liada mentioned. She wanted to know what her choices were before she committed to something for the rest of her life.

That night, the shadowrunners gathered at Lothan's place once more. Assembled in the troll mage's study, they went over the information they'd gathered and the plans for the run. Jackie Ozone was present again via the Matrix, her anime princess persona on the screen of the telecom sitting on Lothan's desk. The other runners attended in person. Kellan noticed that Orion still refused to mix with the rest of the team.

G-Dogg greeted Kellan warmly when he arrived, and asked her how her lessons were going.

"Learned how to turn people into frogs yet, kid?" he asked, and Kellan wondered briefly if mages could really do that. She'd have to look it up or ask Lothan later.

"Not yet," she said.

"First, I think I'll need to teach her some of the basics," Lothan interjected. "Like lighting candles with something smaller than a blowtorch." The troll chuckled and Kellan blushed.

"Hey, there's times when a blowtorch can come in handy," G-Dogg replied with a wink at Kellan.

Lothan started on one side of the room and asked each runner for their progress report.

Jackie Ozone went first. The decker flashed information on the screen as she went over what she'd learned.

"I confirmed the data that we got from our Mr. Johnson," Jackie said. "The shipment route looks legit and takes our target along the East Road into the metroplex, right along the border of the Redmond Barrens." A map showed up on the screen, and a red line traced out the route along it.

"The security complement for a shipment like this should be Ares standard, which means they'll be well-trained and armed, but we shouldn't face any heavy cyberware or magical support. We can expect at least four guards, plus a driver. Probably AK-97s or SMGs and sidearms, maybe tasers or stun batons for dealing with the riffraff, since they are passing by the Barrens."

"We pinpointed a good spot for things to go down," Silver Max said, and the map on the telecom screen shifted to show a satellite photo image of the highway. It zoomed in on a section of roadway and enlarged to show more detail.

"There's an underpass right before the target site," the dwarf rigger continued, "which provides us with some cover and high ground if we need it. There's enough junk along the edges of the road to provide some additional cover, though no place to hide vehicles unless we park 'em right along the side of the road, which might tip off our targets."

"Liada and I have examined the ether of that area and the surrounding region," Lothan announced, "and, while it's by no means entirely clear of astral detritus, it should pose no difficulties against our own abilities."

"Which means that we're in the clear magic-wise," Liada offered helpfully.

"What about the locals?" Lothan asked.

G-Dogg spoke up. "I did some checking around. Seems like the Red Hot Nukes and the Rusted Stilettos have had a couple of dustups recently, but not much as far south and east as we'll be. Most everyone is talking about the Spikes getting more aggressive along I-5, but their territory is far enough west that they shouldn't be any trouble. So long as word about the shipment doesn't leak to the Nukes, I don't think we have anything to worry about, and everything I've heard says they don't have a clue."

"And we should keep it that way," Lothan said. He paused for a moment. "We could always make certain that the Nukes are out of the way. . . ." he mused aloud.

"How?" G-Dogg asked.

"Perhaps the Ancients could be persuaded to provide a bit of a . . . distraction?" the troll asked.

Everyone turned to look at Orion. The elf ganger glanced at the shadowrunners and shrugged slightly.

"Maybe. What's in it for us?" he asked.

"That's an interesting question," Lothan relied with a tight smile. "But one that I won't ask if you don't. The real question is: how badly do the Ancients want this to go well?"

Orion failed to hide that he was a bit taken aback by how efficiently Lothan turned the tables on him.

"I can ask," was all the elf said.

"Excellent," Lothan replied. "In either case, it doesn't seem that the local rabble will pose much of a problem."

"Bring it on," the Street Deacon said, flexing one of his skeletal chrome hands with a faint whirring noise. "As it is, it doesn't sound like this will be much of a challenge."

"I prefer to find my challenges elsewhere," Lothan said lightly. "The smoother and faster our business goes, the sooner it will be taken care of and we will all get paid."

"Depriving Ares of a measure of their ill-gotten gains is enough for me," the Deacon said, though he clearly wasn't refusing the nuyen the runners would make.

"Speaking of which," Jackie Ozone interjected, "nothing online to indicate that there's anything unusual about this particular shipment."

"Nothing that I've heard, either," the Street Deacon agreed. "Though my eyes and ears within Ares are not what they once were."

"Jackie, what about the cargo?" G-Dogg asked. "What are we lifting?"

"An interesting question," the decker replied. "The manifest says it's a shipment of electronics: tridplayers, cable hardware, drek like that."

"Why would anybody pay to lift a shipment like that?" Kellan asked, speaking up for the first time. "I mean, it can't be worth much more in street value than what the Johnson is paying." A couple of the other shadowrunners smiled knowingly.

"That's the point, kid," G-Dogg replied. "It probably means the manifest is faked and Ares doesn't want Metroplex Customs or the NAN authorities to know what they're moving across the border. They're moving something else with this shipment as a front, but our Mr. Johnson found out about it and wants to nab it. If Ares really is interested in keeping it a secret, then they won't raise a stink if their shipment suddenly goes missing, since it wasn't supposed to be anything all that valuable in the first place. It's not like they can go to Lone Star and complain that somebody stole their contraband."

"Still, it means that we're dealing with an unknown in the form of our cargo," Lothan said. "We'll have to be careful how we handle it. I don't like unknowns." The other shadowrunners only nodded in response.

"All right, then," Lothan said. "Given that information, let's walk through the entire plan. Unless there's anything else . . . ?

"Right, then. Kellan, your part in the plan takes place at the very beginning, and depends entirely on how helpless you can appear."

Kellan didn't like the sound of that one bit.

9

How the frag did I let myself get talked into this? Kellan wondered as she sat in the driver's seat of the little electric three-wheeler. She glanced for about the thousandth time down the darkened stretch of highway that ran along the border between Redmond and Renton, heading into Bellevue. Most of the streetlights along that length of I-90 had been blown out over the years as part of target practice for go-gangs, wizzer-kids and other vandals. The few remaining cast a dim blue-white glow over the roadway. The ferrocrete barriers along either side did their best to separate the East Road from the desolation surrounding it, but some of them were badly in need of repair or missing altogether. The lanes of the highway stretched off into the darkness in either direction as far as Kellan could see.

She spotted approaching headlights and tensed, her hand immediately going to the stun baton hidden under her jacket. The glow of the lights flared brightly for a moment, then they zoomed past, the vehicle not even slowing down. As the red glow of the car's taillights receded into the distance, Kellan reminded herself that the car she was in looked like a junker abandoned alongside the road. For all she knew, Silver Max had found it here and just appropriated it for the run. She had to admit that didn't seem likely, though, since the car still had all its interior furnishings, even if it didn't run.

"How you doing, Kellan?" Jackie Ozone's voice sounded in Kellan's ear through the tiny speaker-and-throat-mic device she wore. It sounded like the decker was sitting right next to her when, in fact, Kellan had no idea where Jackie was. She could be somewhere in the plex or hanging out in the Hong Kong or Denver data havens for all Kellan knew.

She put her fingers to her ear for a moment. "Just wizard," she told Jackie in a tone that said she was getting tired of waiting, then glanced out at the road again.

Silver Max's crisp tone broke into the channel. "Target has passed checkpoint one," he said. "They're on their way. It's showtime, people."

Kellan immediately threw the little electric car into

neutral and made sure the emergency brake was off as G-Dogg and the Street Deacon emerged from the shadows alongside the road. She opened the driver's side door and hopped out. The ork and the street samurai began pushing the little car out into the road. It rolled smoothly, though Kellan could hear a faint whine of cybernetics from the Deacon, so she knew it was costing them some effort.

"We should have gotten Lothan to do this," the Deacon muttered, just loud enough for G-Dogg and Kellan to hear him.

"Lothan doesn't do the heavy work," G-Dogg replied mirthlessly, "that's why he became a mage." The ork flashed Kellan a tusky grin and she smiled back.

They got the three-wheeler positioned nearly in the middle of the road, just a bit askew and facing west toward downtown Seattle. Kellan could see the bright lights and high towers of the city off in the distance, against the gray-black of a cloudy sky. As G-Dogg and the Deacon stopped the car, Kellan hopped in through the open door and put it into park.

Suddenly, the Street Deacon pulled a heavy blade the length of Kellan's forearm from a sheath strapped to his left thigh. Without warning, he plunged the knife into the front passenger side tire of the car.

There was a pop and a hiss of escaping air as he slashed the tire open, then he went and did the same to the rear tire on that side.

"We should make it look good," he said by way of explanation to Kellan and G-Dogg, sheathing the blade.

"Checkpoint two," Silver Max said over the commlink, and the Street Deacon immediately headed for the shadows along the side of the road. G-Dogg took a few steps backward, looking at Kellan where she sat with the driver's side door still open.

"All set?" he asked. Kellan nodded. The ork gave her a thumbs-up and then followed the Street Deacon into the shadows, saying into his throat mike, "We're good to go here. Our damsel is in distress."

"Final check," Jackie Ozone said over the link. "If you're not ready to run, speak now or forever hold your peace." There was a moment of silence, then the decker said, "All right, let's do this."

"Kellan," Silver Max said. "You be ready to ditch if it looks like they're not going to stop."

"No problem," Kellan replied. "I'm not planning on getting run down by a cargo rig today."

"I'll give you as much warning as I can," the dwarf rigger replied, with a note of genuine concern in his voice.

"Thanks," she said. Then she spotted headlights in the distance. "Visual contact," she said into the link.

"Okay, people, keep the chatter to a minimum," Jackie said to everyone. The decker was monitoring the team's communications and those of the Ares personnel, along with the emergency channels and Lone Star bands, for any signs of trouble. She would ensure that the team was alerted to potential interference, and that they would be undisturbed for as long as possible.

The bright lights were getting closer. Kellan could see two sets of headlights; it looked like a smaller truck was leading the larger cargo hauler by a short distance. Kellan kept the driver's side door open a crack, her hand tensed on the handle. If the driver of the lead truck didn't see her in time to stop . . .

The lights drew closer and the lead truck began to slow. Kellan let out a breath she hadn't realized she was holding as both trucks began to brake, their headlights washing over the little electric runabout stalled in the middle of the road. If they decided to simply drive around it, things would get a little more complicated for the runners. When the trucks began to slow down, Kellan hopped out of the car and ran around the front of it, so she was clearly visible in the harsh glow of the halogen lights. She began jumping up and down and waving to get their attention, acting like the stranded motorist she appeared to be.

"Hey!" she yelled. "Help!"

The lead truck banked a bit as it approached, but Kellan quickly realized that the team had planned things out just right. Although the smaller truck could get past her car, the cargo hauler would have to literally push the stalled vehicle out of the way to pass. So the lead truck turned a bit to the side and then came to a stop only a few meters from where Kellan was standing. The cargo hauler's brakes whined as it rolled to a stop a short distance away.

The windows of the lead truck were tinted, and she recalled Lothan's lesson about magicians needing line of sight to affect something with a spell. Smoked, tinted and mirrored windows had become common since the Awakening, primarily in an effort to protect against the threat of criminal magicians. Even if Kellan knew spells to affect the personnel in the truck, she couldn't cast them so long as they were inside.

She waited expectantly, doing her best to look helpless and trying not to think about the stun baton tucked into the inside pocket of her jacket, or the small, snub-nosed pistol G-Dogg had handed her before they left on the run with the comment, "Hopefully, you won't need this." Kellan hoped if she pretended the weapons weren't there, the corporate personnel wouldn't notice them. If they did, Kellan wasn't looking forward to using them.

The passenger side door of the escort vehicle

opened up and a dark-clad figure got out. He came around the front of the truck, moving toward Kellan. She could see he was human, wearing dark coveralls that revealed the bulk of armor padding across his chest and shoulders. He wore a cap with the Ares logo and his eyes gleamed a bit in the light spilling from the trucks' headlights, probably implants automatically adjusting for the light level, since he didn't squint when he looked at her. He wore a pistol in a holster at his waist, and Kellan noticed the flap was open, though he hadn't drawn his weapon . . . yet.

"You all right?" he asked Kellan in a Midwestern drawl that reminded her of Kansas City.

"I—I need some help," Kellan replied. "My car broke down and my phone's dead. Do you have a phone I can use or something?"

"Wait right there, miss," the man said, remaining near the front of the truck and not coming any closer. "I can call to get you a tow."

Kellan took a couple steps forward. "That'd be great! Do you need my credstick or anything?" She began reaching toward her jacket pocket innocently.

"Please stay right there, miss," the man said in a more authoritative tone. "Please remain by your vehicle." Kellan saw the guard's hand stray toward his gun and decided to keep her hands by her side and in plain view.

"Okay," she said, "no problem," and the guard reached up with his left hand to unclip a small mic from the shoulder strap of his uniform.

Kellan focused her gaze on the guard's commlink as Lothan had taught her, and suddenly everything went unnaturally still and quiet. She felt the heat across her skin and narrowed her eyes, focusing, directing the energy outward, and projecting it with all of her concentration. There was a roaring in her ears like a crackling fire and she felt the heat leave her in a rush.

The guard's commlink burst into flames. The man yelled in surprise and shock and immediately dropped the chunk of burning plastic and electronics, forgetting that it was still tethered to his uniform. It slapped against his chest and he tried to beat out the flames with one gloved hand. Kellan was aware of the doors of both trucks flying open.

"Kellan, get down!" a voice in her ear said, and Kellan dropped to the pavement as bullets flew overhead. G-Dogg and the Street Deacon popped up from their hidden positions alongside the road, firing at the surprised Ares guards. The guy Kellan burned didn't even reach his sidearm before a round caught him, spinning him around and dropping him to the ground beside the truck. Another guard came out of the driver's side of the truck, taking cover behind the open door as bullets sparked and ricocheted off the obviously armored vehicle. Men were emerging from the cab of the cargo hauler as well.

Kellan seized the opportunity to make a run for the front of the escort vehicle. She kept low as shots *whang*ed off the pavement nearby. As she rounded the front, she saw that the guard who'd spoken to her was still conscious, fumbling for his sidearm. His armor must have blunted some of the force of the shot that hit him. Kellan was faster, and jammed her stun baton into the man's side. There was an electric sizzle and he cried out, then lay on the ground, twitching slightly.

Kellan looked up just as the rear passenger door of the truck opened up and another man jumped out. She dropped her stun baton and immediately reached for her pistol, moving far too slow, as the Ares guard raised his own gun and Kellan found herself looking down a black barrel that for a moment loomed as large as a train tunnel in her vision. Then there was the sound of tearing cloth and a surprised grunt of pain from the guard as the gun fell from his hands and he crumpled. Orion stood over the fallen body, a bloody sword in his right hand, a matte black pistol in the other.

Before Kellan could even say thanks, a bright flash of light and a boom of thunder jerked her eyes to the cloudy sky. The last fraggin' thing they needed was a sudden rainstorm.

"Dammit," Liada cursed over the commlink. "They've got a fraggin' storm spirit!" There was another flash of light, brighter than before. Kellan saw a streak of lightning come from the direction of the other truck. It struck along the side of the road with a rolling boom of thunder, sending up a cloud of sparks and a shower of debris.

"We're pinned down!" G-Dogg shouted. The lightning bolt had struck very close to his position.

"On it!" Liada replied.

Orion gestured at Kellan with the point of his sword, clearly indicating that he wanted her to stay put, then the elf ganger slipped around to the rear of the truck. He looked carefully around it, then disappeared around the corner.

Fraggit if I'm going to just stand here! Kellan thought. She followed close behind Orion.

The Ares guards with the cargo hauler were hunkered down close to the truck's heavy cab, firing their guns in the direction of G-Dogg and the Street Deacon. Hovering above the truck was a large, roiling mass of black clouds. Blue-white electricity shimmered between the clouds, and Kellan thought she could see a great, black-feathered bird with eyes of burning electric blue in the storm. A harsh, cold wind blew from the clouds. *A storm spirit,* Kellan remembered Liada saying. She had never seen one before.

She couldn't see Liada or Lothan, though she knew

the two mages had to be close at hand and within line of sight of their target. Liada said they were going to handle the storm spirit, although Kellan had no idea exactly how. She heard a cry of pain from the guard on the opposite side of the truck, but no shot, so she assumed Orion had struck again. Then one of the Ares guards beside the cargo hauler fired a few shots toward Orion, which forced Kellan to duck back behind the end of the escort vehicle. She clutched her own pistol in both hands, listening to the sounds of the gunfire and the crackling of thunder on the opposite side.

"Max," Lothan said over the link, "we need a distraction out in front of the main truck."

"Roger," the dwarf rigger replied. There was a high-pitched whine of rotors and Kellan saw a drone swoop out of the darkness toward the cargo hauler. It looked like a small flying garbage can and was about the right size, except with a collar of rotor blades around the uppermost edge and a chin-mounted machine gun below. Its cylindrical surface was covered in heavy armor plates.

The drone opened up with its machine gun, tracing a chattering arc of fire along the pavement just in front of the cab of the cargo hauler, sending up sparks and ricochets from the road where the high-caliber rounds struck. The security guards scrambled for cover. Then the drone swiveled its gun up toward the hovering storm spirit and ripped off another burst directly into it. Tongues of flame shot from the barrel of the gun, but if the spirit was affected by the gunfire in the slightest, it didn't show it.

It was the distraction Lothan asked for, and Kellan was going to take full advantage of it. Staying low to the ground, she hustled along the side of the road toward the cargo hauler, making her way around to the back of it. Silver Max's drone veered off as the Ares guards opened fire on it. She heard some rounds ricochet off the drone's armor, but it simply withdrew a short distance away, hovering off to the side of the road, the guards still well within the range of its machine gun, but where they would have a difficult time returning fire. Another sustained burst of machine-gun fire roared in the dark, forcing the guards to keep their heads down, though Kellan noticed Max wasn't shooting directly at them. That might disable the truck, which would pretty much frag their whole run.

Kellan reached the back of the truck and crouched there, listening. She could hear a low droning chant coming from the back of the truck, a kind of singsong in a language she didn't recognize, and she felt a tingle along her skin, the hairs on the back of her neck bristling. *Magic.* She was sure of it.

She glanced up at the side rigging of the truck's cargo area, then grabbed one of the cargo straps and pulled herself up, trying to move silently. Then she dropped the strap from one hand and grabbed her pistol with the other as she swung around into the back of the truck, bringing her gun up to cover the interior.

Nestled among the heavy plastic packing crates in the back of the truck was a thin figure wearing a long, dark coat. Her hair was long and braided, and it looked like she had at least some Native blood. She turned as Kellan landed and raised one hand, a faint shimmer forming around it. Kellan squeezed the trigger twice, snapping off a couple shots. The first one went wide, blowing a hole in a crate with a scattering of packing material. The second hit the shaman in her shoulder, spinning her to the side into one of the crates and breaking her concentration. The spell, whatever it had been, didn't go off.

Kellan moved closer, gun held extended in both hands, leveled at the shaman as she struggled to her feet. It looked like her coat was lined with enough armor that it stopped the bullet, although Kellan knew from experience that it still felt like being hit with a baseball bat wielded by a troll. The shaman had suffered some blunt trauma to be sure, maybe worse. She was clutching at her shoulder as she regained her feet.

"Try that again," Kellan said flatly, "and the next one goes between your eyes."

The shaman glared at her, but didn't say anything, slowly lowering her hands to her sides, but keeping them where Kellan could see them.

"You're controlling the spirit out there," Kellan said, and the shaman nodded.

"Get rid of it," Kellan told her, raising her gun slightly for emphasis. "And don't try pulling anything, understand?"

The shaman paused for a moment, eyes locked on Kellan's, and Kellan wondered if she was using magic to try to figure out if she was bluffing. She didn't feel anything, but it was hard to tell. Then the shaman slowly raised her hands and began to chant like she had before. Kellan could feel the magic in the air, could almost see it coalescing around the other woman.

The spell lashed out at Kellan, hitting her like a physical blow. She reflexively pushed against it, gritting her teeth and holding her ground. It felt like icy claws were tearing at her very soul, but she thought about the crystalline egg Lothan had taught her to visualize, and the claws seemed to scrape against it without really hurting her. At the same time, her finger squeezed the trigger.

The shaman just looked at Kellan, shocked that her spell had failed, then she doubled over when the shot hit her in the gut and crumpled to the deck of the truck. The effects of the spell faded with her, and

Kellan gasped as time seemed to snap back to normal. She felt a bit drained, but her adrenaline was pumping and her heart was pounding. Kellan stared at the fallen shaman for a moment, but she didn't move. Kellan keyed her commlink.

"This is K," she said. "I'm in the back of the truck. Their shaman is down."

"Good work," Lothan replied. "That's definitely taken the fight out of the storm spirit as well as their magical defenses. Let's wrap this up, shall we?" the troll mage said to no one in particular.

Kellan felt another surge of magic, like a rippling in the air, and the gunfire ahead of the truck suddenly fell silent. She heard a clang of metal and a cry of pain from the right side of the truck cab, then suddenly Liada and Orion swung into the back of the truck from opposite sides. The Street Deacon and Lothan followed close behind.

The other shadowrunners quickly searched the back of the truck for any other Ares personnel, then Lothan spoke into his commlink.

"Max, we're clear," he said.

"Roger," the dwarf rigger replied. "I'm on my way."

"Jackie, status," the troll said.

"We've got a window," the decker said in a businesslike tone, her previous playfulness absent. "A call went out to Lone Star when things started going down, but I'm scrambling some messages from the dispatch that should keep them busy for a little while. You've got five, maybe ten minutes at the outside."

"All right, let's go," Lothan told the rest of the team.

Liada hunkered down beside the fallen shaman, looking her over. There was blood on the flatbed.

"Is she . . . ?" Kellan asked and Liada shook her head.

"Not yet," she said.

"Dump her," Lothan told the Street Deacon. The street samurai holstered his weapon to scoop up the unconscious shaman. He tossed her off the end of the truck onto the street. Kellan started to say something, but a glance from Liada made her reconsider it. The elf mage shook her head slightly.

Orion hopped down from the back of the truck, sheathing his sword. He disappeared around the corner as Silver Max and G-Dogg climbed into the cab of the cargo hauler. The engine roared to life again and Lothan grabbed hold of one of the straps holding the crates in place.

"Let's ride!" G-Dogg called from the cab. Silver Max threw the truck into gear and it lurched forward, forcing the shadowrunners in back to grab for handholds. Max plowed past the escort truck and the electric three-wheeler, and Kellan could see security guards lying scattered across the road. Some lay in dark puddles of blood, while others appeared completely unmarked. There was no one to watch as the truck, its cargo and the shadowrunners rumbled away down the highway and into the night.

10

With Jackie Ozone running interference in the Matrix, the shadowrunners were gone long before Lone Star responded to the scene of the hijacking. The decker fed the team a running update of the response to their activity, but it was clear they'd made a clean getaway. Lone Star had started a search, but the team planned on concluding their business long before the authorities had any chance of finding them.

Silver Max took the first exit off the highway and headed into Redmond. The rigger expertly guided the big truck through the dark maze of streets, lined with the burned-out shells of cars and other refuse—living and nonliving. If anyone noticed an Ares cargo hauler trucking through the streets so late at night, they didn't bother doing anything about it. People in the Barrens generally knew to mind their own business. It wasn't healthy to do otherwise.

Lothan talked in low tones over the commlink, presumably with Jackie, although Kellan couldn't be sure. The troll mage used a private channel. The number of turns and back roads Silver Max took them on convinced Kellan the dwarf must have an implanted global positioning system. He navigated the streets of the Barrens like they were tattooed on the back of his hand. *Or maybe the inside of his skull is more like it,* Kellan thought.

In fairly short order, the truck pulled up outside of what used to be part of an old strip mall, built around a central anchor store with a sizable loading dock, which was ideal for their purposes. G-Dogg hopped down from the cab to haul open the rusty garage door, which protested this movement, and allow the truck to pull inside. Orion roared up on the back of his Yamaha Rapier right behind them, pulling the bike inside as G-Dogg pulled the door closed. The Street Deacon jumped down from the back of the truck to help, and the two of them wrestled the corrugated metal door closed as Silver Max killed the truck's engine and switched off the headlights.

The abandoned loading area was plunged into darkness, the only illumination the dim light coming through the heavy sheets of plastic covering the few windows. Kellan waited for her eyes to adjust to the gloom. Everyone else on the team was either a meta-human or—in the Street Deacon's case—had cyber-netic eyes and could see in near-total darkness. Kellan couldn't even think about replacing her eyes without feeling nauseous. She blinked a few times, and was able to make out the shadowy shapes of the other runners around her.

"Looks like we're in the clear," Jackie reported over the commlink. "I'll continue to keep watch and let you know if there's any trouble."

"Understood. Good work, Jackie," Lothan replied. "Well, then," he said, turning to the rest of the team. "Now we await Mr. Johnson and our payment. G-Dogg, why don't you, Deacon and Orion keep a look-out for the arrival of our employer." Although phrased politely, it wasn't a request, and G-Dogg nodded, moving off to get the other two men and comply.

"Good job with that shaman," Liada said to Kellan as she tucked her gear into her ever-present shoul-der bag.

"But not exactly according to plan," Lothan inter-jected, giving Kellan a disapproving glance. "You were supposed to stay with the decoy vehicle."

"And what, get shot?" Kellan said.

"Not if you stayed under cover."

"Lay off her, Lothan," Liada challenged the big troll. "She did a good job taking out that shaman. Saved us a lot of trouble."

Lothan bristled. "I would have dealt with her and her spirit soon enough."

"Of course," Liada sneered. "But not as fast as Kellan did. We could have overcome that shaman's defenses together, but thanks to her we didn't have to bother. One stun blast took the rest of those guards down like that"—she snapped her fingers—"and we were on our way."

"Success doesn't excuse excess," the troll shot back. He took a step toward Kellan. "In the future, if you can't stick to the plan, you will at least inform everyone else of your movements. Don't go off on your own, or you're liable to end up in the line of fire." Then he turned on his heel and stalked to the end of the truck, clambering down with the aid of his heavy, gnarled staff.

"Makkanagee," Liada muttered under her breath, watching him go. Then she turned toward Kellan. "Don't listen to him," she said. "You did good. Lothan just hates it when somebody comes up with a good idea that he can't take the credit for." Liada flashed Kellan a smile and touched her arm. "Hey, you okay?" she asked, realizing that Kellan's face had gone white as she holstered her pistol. Kellan's hands were starting to shake and she folded her arms

across her chest, hugging them close to get them to stop.

"Yeah, yeah," she said. "Fine."

"It's just post-run shakes," Liada said sympathetically. "Coming down from the rush. You'll be okay."

"It's just, I never . . ." Kellan began, glancing up at Liada and then looking down again, embarrassed to say more to the more experienced shadowrunner.

"What? Shot anyone?"

"Not like that," Kellan replied quietly. "I mean, I shot *at* people when I was running in KC. Probably even hit some," she snorted mirthlessly. "But I never shot somebody that close before, right in front of me. It wasn't like this in Kansas City."

"Get used to it," Liada said, and a note in her voice made Kellan look up at her. The elf woman's face was sympathetic, but also cold. "She was working for a corp. She knew the risks. She won't be the last one, Kellan, not in this biz. If you're lucky, you'll at least get to be face-to-face with everyone you have to shoot. It's when you start shooting them in the back that you need to worry."

Liada laid a hand on her shoulder, and then left Kellan alone with her thoughts. The run kept playing in her head like a simsense loop; the moment when the shaman tried to cast that spell on her, the feel of the gun in her hand, the look on the shaman's face when the spell didn't work and Kellan's bullet caught her in the gut. Kellan wondered if she'd survived, or if she had died on the highway before help arrived. She wondered if that was how she was going to go one day.

She knew the risks. Liada's words came back to her. She knew that's the way it was in the shadows: kill or be killed, survival of the fittest. When you didn't have the advantages of wealth and privilege, or even the legal existence granted by a SIN, the other option was to be like those lost souls they passed in the Barrens on the way here: squatting in abandoned ruins, living like rats, victims of the corporate machine. Kellan knew she could never live like that.

Looking at the crate she was leaning against, she wondered what it was that they had gone to all this trouble to acquire. Crouching down, she read the shipping label. Most of the information consisted of barcodes for electronic readers to scan, but the words made Kellan frown. She checked the labels on some of the other crates and they were basically the same. Then she went to the front of the cargo area and found a pry bar she used to open one of the crates, popping the lid to look inside. It confirmed what the label on the outside said, meaning that the contents of the other crates were probably the same, not some sort of blind for contraband or hidden cargo. But then why would anyone—?

"What the frag do you think you're doing?"

Kellan jumped and turned to see Orion gracefully pulling himself up onto the back of the truck, glaring at her.

"I'm just checking. . . ." she began, but the elf strode forward, grabbing the pry bar from her hand.

"Nobody told you to check anything," he said in a low, harsh tone.

"Yeah, well, somebody should," Kellan shot back. "Why the frag is our Johnson paying for a shipment of electronic drek that he could buy at any mall in the plex?"

"What?" Orion said.

"See for yourself," Kellan replied, gesturing toward the open crate. "Simdecks, players, interface cables, blank chips—it's all Hong Kong–grade electronics, not even top-of-the-line Novatech or Mitsuhama stuff."

Orion gripped the edge of the open crate, peering inside with a look of disbelief visible even in the dim light. He cursed under his breath, then stalked off with deliberate purpose in his stride, jumping down from the back of the truck. Kellan quickly followed, in case he was going to Lothan to complain about her.

She saw G-Dogg escort "Mr. Johnson" inside. Their employer was alone, and dressed much the same as the first time Kellan saw him, in dark, nondescript clothing that shouted class and influence. He approached Lothan and the two of them began talking in low tones. Orion pulled up short when he saw the troll mage speaking with Mr. Johnson. There was a dark scowl on the elf's face. He folded his arms and waited as Lothan and the other man concluded their business.

Kellan went to stand with Liada and G-Dogg. Silver Max still sat in the cab of the truck. Kellan couldn't make out what Lothan and Mr. Johnson were saying to each other, but it seemed clear that the other man was happy with what he was hearing. Lothan gestured somewhat grandly toward the truck, but the Johnson waved a dismissal, making it clear that he felt no need to inspect their prize.

"Lothan's probably telling him how he pulled it off all by himself," Liada whispered.

"As long as the cred's good," G-Dogg replied.

Kellan looked away from Lothan when she saw movement in her peripheral vision. The Street Deacon entered the garage, walking toward the truck. The street samurai reached the cab and stopped dead in his tracks, staring at Lothan and their Mr. Johnson. Kellan swore that the man's face blanched as pale as the white skull tattoo he wore. His hands flexed as if grasping for something unseen.

"What's with the Deacon?" she asked quietly, and G-Dogg glanced in that direction. The Street Deacon quickly regained his composure and made his way slowly toward the back of the truck, his eyes on Mr. Johnson the whole time.

"Beats the frag out of me," the ork shrugged. "Who knows what's ever up with him?" He turned his attention back to Lothan and Mr. Johnson. Mr. Johnson took out a handful of credsticks and handed them to the troll, who inspected them and seemed satisfied. They shook hands, and Mr. Johnson walked away as Lothan came over to Kellan, G-Dogg and Liada.

"So?" the ork asked. Kellan noticed that Lothan seemed particularly pleased with himself.

"Payment, as agreed," he pronounced, flourishing the credsticks. "Plus a bonus. Mr. Johnson has said that he has no further need of the cargo, so long as Ares is deprived of it, so we are free to dispose of it as we see fit. That should net us a tidy little sum."

"What is it?" Liada asked.

"Electronics, entertainment centers, stuff like that," Kellan said before Lothan could reply, earning her a withering glare from the troll that asked how she knew this information. Kellan did her best to not quail in front of it.

"Not bad," G-Dogg said, ignoring the exchange of looks. "I know some people who'd be interested and would give us a decent price."

The mention of further profit distracted Lothan

from glaring at Kellan. "Arrange it," he said to the ork. "We should be all right keeping the swag here for a while, but I want to make sure that we haven't scored a lure that will bring Ares security down on us." Then he headed over toward the cab of the truck to fill in the others.

"Well," G-Dogg said to Kellan and Liada. "I've got to make some calls, then I think a little celebration is in order. The night isn't over yet, we're still alive and, for the moment, we're flush with nuyen. What do you say to hitting Dante's Inferno or Penumbra?"

"Sounds good to me," Liada replied, glancing at Kellan.

"Wizard," she agreed, though she wasn't feeling as good as G-Dogg obviously was about the whole thing.

"Let's invite Max," G-Dogg said, and he and Liada followed Lothan toward the truck. Kellan looked around for Orion and saw that he had stopped Mr. Johnson by the side door of the garage. She wanted to catch the elf before he buzzed, so she decided to interrupt.

". . . promised us those weapons, Brickman," Orion was saying as Kellan approached. At a glance from Mr. Johnson, Orion broke off as Kellan got closer.

"Um . . . hey," she said, glancing from one man

to the other. "We were going to go out, have a few," she said to Orion. "Just wanted to tell you that you're welcome to come with."

"My business here isn't finished," the elf said coldly, glaring at the other man.

"Oh, okay." Kellan backed away, then turned and walked toward the truck as quickly as possible without running. G-Dogg, Max and Liada were waiting for her next to the cab.

"What's with that?" G-Dogg asked her, nodding in the direction of Orion and the man he called Brickman. The two men continued to talk, then Brickman gestured politely toward the door and Orion walked out ahead of him, his back stiff with anger.

"Dunno," Kellan said slowly, watching them go.

"Well, the Deacon is going to take first shift watching our haul," Liada said, "and Lothan already took off. It's late for a guy his age," she continued with a vicious little smirk. "But he handed over our cut of the cred. Here's yours," and she handed Kellan a credstick.

Kellan took the nuyen with a surge of pride. It felt good to get a cut of the take in addition to the lessons from Lothan. She felt like she really had contributed to the success of the run, and getting paid made it official: she was a shadowrunner in the big time!

"Thanks," Kellan said.

"You earned it," Liada replied with a smile.

"So what are we waiting for?" G-Dogg asked the others with a grin. "Let's party!"

11

Dante's Inferno was not only one of the finest nightclubs in the entire Seattle Metroplex, but also the largest and most impressive nightclub Kellan had ever seen, dwarfing even the industrial splendor and glitz of Underworld 93. G-Dogg led Kellan, Liada and Silver Max up to the front of the usual long line of wannabes waiting to get in, ignoring the jeers of those who considered themselves better candidates for admission. Neolux signs proclaimed the club's name in ten-foot-high flaming letters, announcing NINE CIRCLES OF ACTION! inside. A massive troll, looking dapper in a tailored black tux, guarded the door.

"Newt, my man," G-Dogg said to the troll, who stood behind the velvet rope across the entrance of the club. "Zappinin'?"

The troll smiled broadly, showing blunt lower tusks and one gold-capped tooth.

"Hey, G-Dogg," he rumbled in an improbably low bass. "Same ol' same ol', you know? How 'bout you?"

G-Dogg produced his credstick with a flourish and a wicked smile. "Score!" he said. "Business is good and I'm lookin' to share the wealth." The two metahumans exchanged what appeared to be a stylized handshake, but the gesture actually allowed G-Dogg to unobtrusively slide his credstick into the reader Newt wore around his wrist, mostly hidden under his jacket. There was a barely perceptible beep, nearly drowned out by the music pounding inside the club, and the troll rubbed his hand across his chin, glancing briefly down at his wrist and then smiling broadly.

"Always a pleasure doin' business with you, Dogg," he said, reaching for the rope. Then he nodded at Kellan. "Who's the new kid?"

"Newt, this is Kellan. Kellan, this is Newt, the *second*-best bouncer in all of Seattle, right after me." G-Dogg winked at Kellan as he said it.

"Nice to meetcha," the troll said proffering a huge hand that entirely engulfed Kellan's as she shook it.

"Likewise," she said.

"You ever get tired of hangin' with this ugly trog

and want to see where the *real* action in the plex is, you come talk to me, 'kay?"

"Thanks," Kellan said with a smile. "I'll do that."

"Have fun," Newt said, pulling aside the velvet rope for the shadowrunners to enter, ignoring the complaints of the people waiting in line.

"Pipe down!" Kellan heard the troll yell above the noise of the crowd as they passed by. "Don't make me get physical with the lot of ya!" Then they stepped through the doors and into the Inferno.

In addition to the traditional words, ABANDON EVERY HOPE, ALL YE WHO ENTER HERE, written in flaming neolux above the main entrance off the foyer, Dante's Inferno clearly held to the motto "nothing succeeds like excess." Everything about the club was clearly designed to be as over-the-top and impressive as possible, and it spared no expense to make one man's vision of the perfect sinful playground a reality. Kellan did her level best not to gawk at sights designed to provoke exactly that reaction. None of the other shadowrunners acted like they even noticed anything unusual. They'd clearly been here before—many times, if G-Dogg was any indication. Kellan was impressed by their casual attitude and tried to compose her own face into a cool, jaded expression.

Past the foyer, the club was a giant cylinder, partitioned into nine levels. Kellan could see at least seven levels looming overhead. The floors were made of transparex, allowing you to look all the way up (or down) through them. Ramps wound along around the outside walls of the building's interior, and a massive spiral staircase speared up through the open shaft that ran through the center of each level. Engulfing the staircase was a holographic display of flames, apparently roaring up from deep beneath the nightclub, filled with ghostly images of mostly nude figures writhing in what looked far more like passion than torment.

Fantastic murals covered the walls of the level they were on, depicting green gardens spread over rolling hills, and trees filled with golden fruit. Kellan noticed many of the trees had snakes curled around the branches or peering out from between the leaves.

"Envy," Liada said into Kellan's ear.

"What?" she asked, startled and a little embarrassed to be caught rubbernecking.

Liada smiled. "Envy," she repeated, nodding toward the murals. "Each of the top seven levels of Dante's is themed on one of the seven deadly sins. There's Envy, Sloth, Greed, Pride, Gluttony, Wrath and, of course, Lust. The club is supposed to be modeled on the nine circles of Hell, but I guess our modern-day Dante didn't find as much to work with there as he wanted, so he mixed his metaphors a little. I think he made Envy the entrance level as a sort of joke on all the people waiting to get in. You can bet those poseurs out there envy us right now."

"There are two more levels below this one," G-Dogg chimed in, "which makes nine altogether, although there's actually ten."

"Which are . . . ?" Kellan asked.

"Purgatory, Perdition and Hell," G-Dogg replied, counting them off on his fingers. "That's where the real biz gets done around here. But we're not here for business tonight. C'mon, let's party!"

Her companions clearly enjoyed introducing Kellan to the myriad pleasures of Dante's Inferno. Most of the upper levels of the club featured dancing to various sorts of music, ranging from the violent speed-thrash on Wrath to the slow and sensual sounds on Lust. There was unlimited food on Gluttony, including outrageously indulgent desserts. There were also what Liada called "glamour snacks"—illusory food created with magic. The food had fantastic flavor and texture, but no actual substance. You could eat it forever and never feel full or absorb a single calorie. Kellan tried an amazing piece of cheesecake with "strawberries from the garden of Paradise," that was the best she'd ever had, even if it wasn't real.

There was a near-infinite variety of drinks, as well. The Inferno's bartenders knew their business, and could not only mix up whatever their customers wanted, but did it with flair. For the indecisive, they suggested concoctions Kellan considered to be the extreme of exotic. G-Dogg bought the first round for everyone on Envy, and they toasted the success of their run, and to more of the same in the future.

Though she was enjoying the company of her new-found friends and the pleasures of the Inferno, there was something at the back of Kellan's mind that prevented her from throwing herself wholeheartedly into the celebration. When they were drinking a round on Pride, Kellan finally decided to say what she was thinking.

"What I don't get," she said above the pulse of the music, "is why that Johnson paid good cred for us to lift a bunch of cheap electronics, only to turn around and give 'em to us. And what was the point of us working with Orion?"

"Frag if I know," G-Dogg said, taking a sip of his drink. Kellan had laughed when she saw that the big, frozen concoction was served in a coconut shell and decorated with a tiny umbrella. "Johnsons do some strange drek sometimes. It's all smoke and mirrors, corporate infighting and politics 'n' stuff."

"Doesn't really matter why," Silver Max chimed in. He was on his third imported ale, which he drank with considerable relish. He wiped his mouth with the back of one hand as he set down his empty mug.

"As long as the Johnson's cred is good, who cares why he wants it done?"

"Just seems weird to me, that's all," Kellan said.

"Get used to it," Liada replied. "Because you're going to see a lot of weirder things in this biz than an employer asking you to do stuff for no good reason."

"But sometimes, don't you want to know *why* a Johnson wants something done?"

Liada shook her head. "Not as long as it doesn't put my hoop on the line. Most of the time you're way better off *not* knowing. The employer is paying for discretion, and that's what he gets."

"The trick is to know when you need to know, if you know what I mean," G-Dogg said with a laugh. "And to know when and what you don't need to know and not know it."

"I *definitely* need another drink," Max said. "G-Dogg is starting to make sense." The dwarf pushed away from the table. "It's my round, what do you all want?" Max signaled for a waitress by waving his credstick above his head.

"I still don't see why we needed Orion on the run," Kellan persisted. G-Dogg shrugged, hooking the miniature umbrella on his tusk as he tipped up the coconut. Liada made a face.

"I don't either," she said, "but he was on the Johnson's tab and he did his job, so I don't care. I'm just glad he's gone. Fraggin' Ancients," she muttered, tossing back the last of her drink.

"What about them?" Kellan asked.

"They're an embarrassment," Liada said. "They put on airs about how they're so much better than norms, than everyone else really, like they're the exiled nobility of Tir Tairngire, or something." The name of the elven homeland rolled off her tongue with an almost musical lilt and an accent Kellan couldn't place. "But they're really just ganger punks, no better than any other gang."

"He definitely had a problem with Mr. Johnson," Kellan said, recalling the obviously hostile conversation between Orion and their employer.

"That's his business," G-Dogg replied.

"I think the Street Deacon knew him, too. The Johnson, I mean."

The ork shrugged. "Coulda been. The Deacon probably worked for him before."

"It seemed like more than that to me," Kellan began. G-Dogg interrupted by banging his cup down on the table and letting out a thunderous belch.

"You're thinkin' about it too much, kid," he said. "It's over and done with. The Johnson got what he wanted and we made out with more cred than we planned. It was a milk run. Orion has a stick shoved sideways up his hoop like most of the Ancients and the Deacon is a fraggin' weirdo, always has been. End of story."

He pushed away from the table and stood up, offering Kellan his hand. "C'mon. I'm up for some dancing. I'll show you some of my moves," he offered her a tusky grin.

Liada stood as well. "Now this I *gotta* see," she said. Kellan glanced at Max, but the dwarf just shook his head.

"Not me," he said, "these legs weren't built for dancin'. I'm just fine where I am." He punctuated the gesture by plucking his new mug of ale off the tray the waitress brought over. "I'll stay and guard the drinks."

"Ha!" G-Dogg snorted. "We expect them to still be here when we get back, halfer."

"Then you better not be gone too long, goblin boy," Max retorted, a smile splitting his bearded face.

Kellan laughed and decided to follow G-Dogg's lead. She put her concerns away, took the ork's hand and headed out onto the dance floor. He was right. Why worry? Now was the time to have some fun.

The celebration lasted well into the night. Kellan didn't remember how she got back to the coffin hotel, though she vaguely recalled something about refusing a ride from G-Dogg or Max to make her own way there. In hindsight, it was a marvel she hadn't been jumped between the street corner and the sealed and locked coffin module. Probably, it was late enough (or early enough) that the nocturnal urban predators were holing up for the coming of dawn. Kellan made no effort to get undressed before collapsing onto the temperform padding and falling deeply asleep.

In her dreams, she relived parts of their run, disjointed images passing through her mind: Orion's catlike moves and the flash of his blade in the darkness, Jackie Ozone's voice speaking in her ear, like the omniscient voice of a spirit guide, the thunder and crackling lightning of the storm spirit. She saw the shocked look on the face of the Ares shaman over and over again as she shot her in slow motion, seeing the shaman lying facedown on the deck of the truck, blood seeping out from underneath her as it hadn't in reality, until Kellan was standing in a puddle of crimson.

She relived their escape and arrival at the abandoned garage, then peeking into the crates to discover they contained only cheap electronics.

"What the frag do you think you're doing?" Orion said from the back of the truck.

Kellan turned to face the angry elf ganger just as someone shot Orion in the back: *Blam! Blam! Blam!* Three quick shots. Orion jerked forward, exit wounds blossoming crimson on the front of his T-shirt, a look of complete shock on his face that transformed his arrogant sneer into almost childlike surprise as he tried to comprehend what had happened. He pitched forward and Kellan ran to the edge of the truck bed to see what was happening.

Mr. Johnson stood there in his nondescript black clothes, dark shades covering his eyes, smoking pistol in his hand. He turned calmly to where Lothan stood nearby and put three shots into the troll mage, who pitched forward like a felled tree. A pool of dark blood spread out on the concrete floor around him. Turning to his left, Mr. Johnson just as calmly shot the Street Deacon before he could draw his guns. The Deacon's dark shades and hat were knocked off as he fell, and he looked surprisingly old and ordinary to Kellan without them, his artificial eyes staring blindly upward in death.

It was like everything was moving in slow motion. The dark-clad man picked off the shadowrunners one by one, leaving them lying dead on the cold concrete floor of the abandoned garage: G-Dogg, Liada and Silver Max, until only Kellan was left. She should have reached for her own gun, or her stun baton, or tried to run and hide, but she couldn't move, couldn't even cry out. She just watched, paralyzed with fear like she'd never known, as Mr. Johnson walked toward her. She heard the electronic whisper of Jackie Ozone in her ear.

"I could have told you this would happen," she said sadly. Then Mr. Johnson raised his gun toward Kellan.

"Nice and tidy," he said, and pulled the trigger.

The bang and flash of the muzzle was the last thing Kellan saw as she jerked awake.

"NO!" she yelled, followed by "Ow!" as her head connected with the low ceiling of the coffin module. She flopped back down, rubbing her head and trying to slow her rapid breathing. Someone in the next module yelled, "Shaddup!" and pounded on the side.

A dream, she thought, breathing deeply, hungrily inhaling the stale, rank air inside the coffin. *Just a dream.*

Or was it? she asked herself, shifting to a sitting position—tough to manage in the confined space. After all, Kellan thought, she *was* supposed to be a magician. Could magicians see the future in their dreams? Liada and G-Dogg had acted like the mage's reading fortunes for people with tarot cards was some kind of scam, but maybe some magicians really could foresee things. And Liada had said that her dreams might have meaning now that her Talent was awakened.

Her fingers rubbed the cool jade of the amulet. What about her artifact? Even Lothan didn't know exactly what the amulet was except for the fact that it was magical in some way. Maybe it had influenced her dreams.

Or maybe it was just a fraggin' dream, Kellan thought with a sigh. A dream brought on by worrying too much and celebrating with a few too many drinks. It could be as simple as that—nothing more than her subconscious working overtime after her first shadowrun with new partners in a new city. Maybe it was nothing more than that.

"But I can't take that chance," Kellan muttered quietly. If there was even a possibility that there was something important surfacing in her dream, she *had* to check it out. Despite G-Dogg's advice to just forget about it, she couldn't put her questions aside so easily. She realized now that she had never even considered that the runs in KC might have been more complex than what she'd seen on the surface. She'd been naive; or maybe her team never graduated from the small stuff.

She settled back onto the padding with a sigh. *I've got to get the frag out of this place.* But her first priority was going to be a little digging about the man Orion called Brickman. She wanted to find out why he was willing to pay to have something hijacked that he didn't want. And she wanted to know why the elf ganger had been along for the ride.

So resolved, Kellan managed to fall back to sleep. Her dreams, if any, troubled her no more that night.

12

After getting a steaming soykaf latte and a dough-nut from the Stuffer Shack on the corner, Kellan settled herself in her sleep coffin, sitting cross-legged on the temperfoam padding, her hair brushing against the ceiling. She took her well-used Fuchi da-taBook out of her bag. The computer had outlasted the company that made it by a few years, and though it was nowhere close to top-of-the-line, it would do until Kellan had a chance to get something better. She'd cut her teeth on the dataBook and the shape of its keyboard was familiar to her fingers. She plugged the small computer into the power and data ports in the coffin, slotting her credstick to start the flow of energy and information. The flatscreen on the wall showed the credit slowly ticking off.

Rolling out the dataBook's flatscreen, she booted

the computer and settled down to surf the Matrix. The trouble with having access to a tremendous amount information was that there was a tremendous amount of information, most of it completely useless. The Matrix was like an ocean of data, wider and deeper than any physical sea. It took a measure of skill, time and patience to sift through the waves of data to find exactly what you were looking for.

Like every other kid who went to school, Kellan had learned about the Internet, the precursor to the Matrix. It had consisted of a mismatched network of slow computers linked by antiquated voice communication systems. The computers required special adaptors just to send data over copper wiring never intended for such use. It was crude, slow and, from the sound of things, not all that useful.

The Crash changed all that. In 2029, a computer virus of unprecedented virulence struck the Internet, wiping out information, corrupting backup systems and even burning out hardware. It spread like wildfire around the world, carried by the interconnectivity of the communications systems, and it devastated the network wherever it went. The virus mutated and adapted to successfully attack new systems as it encountered them. It thwarted every attempt to purge it, infecting every computer with which it came into contact. The world telecommunications system practically collapsed.

Then the United States government activated a top-secret team of cyberspecialists named Echo Mirage. Using cutting-edge neural interface technology, they were able to directly engage and destroy the virus. Though it cost the lives of most of the cybercommandos, the threat was ended.

From the ashes of the Internet arose a new telecommunications grid, designed to take full advantage of digital technology and new optical computing tech. It took years to build it but, by the time Kellan was born, the Matrix had been part of everyday life for almost a generation. She could hardly imagine a world without immediate access to vast amounts of data. All you needed was a computer or a terminal and a place to jack in.

The Matrix created a new breed of computer hackers, called deckers. Just as the hackers in their time embraced the newest tech and used it to advance their own goals, the deckers were those who immediately understood the potential of the Matrix as a treasure trove of information. By plugging themselves directly into the information flow, deckers could move faster, dig deeper and generally circumvent any security system. Shadow deckers made their living surfing through the data waves of the Matrix, like pearl divers going deep to find those few precious gems they could sell to the right buyer.

Kellan wasn't going anywhere near that deep; she

just needed to search for some basic information about their mysterious Mr. Johnson.

She entered the name "Brickman," but the results didn't get her much. There were a number of Brickmans in the Seattle Metroplex Telecom Directory, and none of the listings gave Kellan any clues as to which of them, if any, was the man she was looking for. That was assuming he had a number listed in the directory to begin with. She didn't have a photo for image matching, and the directory wasn't configured to search by physical description.

Kellan thought for a minute. The only other significant piece of information she had about Brickman was his interest in Ares Macrotechnology, and a possible connection with the Ancients. After all, it had been a Ares shipment he'd hired them to take, and he must have cut his deal with Orion—whatever it was—before he'd met with Lothan to finalize the run to acquire the shipment. Also, he obviously had a source for the Ares shipping routes.

She fed the new parameters into the browser and set it to work while she sipped her latte and ate, mulling things over. She wasn't entirely sure what she'd do with the data, if anything turned up. It depended on what Brickman was up to. If she'd learned anything about life in the shadows, it was that trusting your instincts was what kept you alive, and one step ahead of the other guy. And her instincts told

her that she needed to figure out what she was staying ahead of.

Bingo. The browser signaled that it had found
something. Kellan scrolled through the information
on the screen, and her eyebrows rose in surprise.

He works for Ares. She reread the section of the
corporate host that showed one Simon Brickman was
a midlevel manager for Knight Errant Security Services, a wholly owned subsidiary of Ares Macrotechnology, Inc. There was even a tiny photo that
matched the man Kellan had seen at both meets.
Brickman worked for a subsidiary of the company
he'd hired them to steal from! But why?

Kellan did some additional searches, but wasn't
able to turn up much more about Brickman other
than the fact that he'd attended Knight Errant's training academy in Seattle, but had moved into manage-
ment fairly quickly from fieldwork and was
apparently up-and-coming at the company. Why
would a guy like that want to hire shadowrunners
to steal from his own parent company, and then not
even take possession of the swag? Kellan's search
turned up more questions than answers. She tossed
back the last of her drink and closed up the small
computer.

She glanced at the time readout inside the coffin
and saw that most of the afternoon was gone. If she
gave him what she'd learned so far, maybe Lothan

would be able to fill in some of the blanks about what Brickman was up to. She stuffed her gear into her bag and headed out to catch a cab to Lothan's place.

When she got to the house on Capitol Hill, Kellan knocked, but there was no answer. She hadn't even considered that Lothan might be out. Not sure what she hoped to achieve, Kellan turned the doorknob. To her surprise, the door opened, and so she stepped inside, closing it behind her.

She hesitated in the hallway, not sure which room to try first. She heard low voices conversing in Lothan's study, one obviously Lothan's deep bass, and one other she couldn't make out. Kellan took a deep breath and knocked on the closed door. The conversation instantly stopped, and there was a long moment of silence that made Kellan cringe, glancing around the hall for any signs of attack, or a quick escape route, if she needed one. Then the door opened and Lothan stood framed in the doorway, peering down at Kellan with a thunderous expression on his craggy face.

"We are not scheduled for a lesson today, Kellan," the troll growled.

"Um . . . you're right," Kellan stammered, "but I wanted to ask you something. I didn't think about calling before I came. I can ask you later."

"It's all right, Lothan," said a voice in the room.

The troll's expression smoothed out, then he stepped back and gestured to Kellan to enter.

Kellan didn't recognize the woman sitting in one of the chairs by Lothan's desk. She didn't look much older than Kellan, though she had a quiet confidence about her. Kellan immediately noticed that her close-cropped blond hair highlighted the silvery gleam of a datajack at her temple. She wore a close-fitting, sleeveless black T-shirt and black jeans with athletic shoes. A tailored synthleather jacket was draped over the back of the chair.

"Hoi, Kellan," she said in a familiar voice, "nice to see you."

Kellan paused for a moment, trying to place the voice. She was sure that she'd never seen the woman before but she sounded like . . .

"Jackie?" she asked, and the woman smiled, flashing perfect white teeth in the dimness of the room.

"The one and only," she said.

"Consider yourself honored," Lothan said from behind Kellan as he closed the study door. "Only a select few meet the infamous Jackie Ozone in the flesh." There was a playful, mocking familiarity in his tone.

"Infamous?" Jackie said with a smile. "Why, Lothan, you silver-tongued devil. . . ."

"So, what is it you wanted to ask?" Lothan cleared his throat and deftly changed the subject. Kellan fished in her bag for the dataBook, opening it up and tapping the controls before holding it so Lothan could see the roll-out screen.

"Brickman," she said simply. "Our Mr. Johnson. Apparently he works for Ares, or at least for Knight Errant. I'm trying to figure out why he hired us to steal from his own company."

"How did you get this?" Lothan asked, nodding toward the screen and ignoring her unspoken question.

"I came up with a couple of keywords, then did a Matrix search with a good browser," Kellan said.

"That's good basic technique," Jackie complimented her, coming around to look at the screen. She cast a critical eye at the dataBook.

"Apparently we're to have a lesson today, after all," Lothan said with a sigh. "Kellan, I assumed you were experienced enough to know better than to dig around in the background of an employer and then sharing that information indiscriminately."

"Hardly indiscriminately," Jackie interjected. "After all she *does* know us."

Lothan shot the decker a look that clearly said, "stay out of this." "Be that as it may," he continued. "It doesn't change the fact that our employers pay for and expect a certain measure of discretion, as well as professional behavior. If you want to be successful in this business, Kellan, I suggest you keep that in mind."

"Oh, come off it, Lothan!" Jackie scoffed. "It's not like you didn't check out Brickman and learn the same info before you took the job." The troll glared at the decker.

"Then . . . you knew?" Kellan asked. "I mean, you knew Brickman worked for Knight Errant, and you didn't say anything to the rest of us?"

"Of course I knew," Lothan said patiently, like he was explaining the blatantly obvious to a small child. "Only a fool doesn't check out a potential employer's credentials, just to be on the safe side, but the important thing is not to be *seen* prying into an employer's affairs. It's a matter of appearances. I didn't say anything because it didn't concern you."

"Don't you think it's kind of strange—Brickman hiring us to steal from his own company?"

"Not at all. It happens all the time. Midlevel employees become involved in corporate politics or power struggles within their own company, and some find it useful to go outside the corporate structure looking for a little help to move their own agendas forward. I've seen far stranger things in my time."

"But I think Brickman is up to something—"

"Of *course* he is," Lothan interrupted, his patience

obviously wearing thin. "But Mr. Brickman's plans, whatever they may be, are of no concern to us. He hired us for a job, we did the job to his satisfaction, and he paid us the agreed-upon amount—with a nice little bonus, I may add. Now our business is concluded. Whatever Brickman's plans are, they're none of our concern. I suggest you invest whatever money you have left over, after a night of celebration in G-Dogg's company, in some new clothing and whatever other necessities you may need, and be here on time for your next lesson. Forget about Mr. Brickman."

"But . . ."

"Leave it be, Kellan!" the troll rumbled, drawing himself up to his full height to tower head and shoulders above Kellan. "Do I make myself clear?"

"Yeah," she said flatly. "Like crystal."

"Good. Now, if you'll excuse us. . . ." Lothan stared pointedly at the door, and Kellan stuffed the dataBook back into her bag and left without another word, just a backward glance at Jackie and Lothan before she closed the door behind her.

Fraggin' know-it-all! Kellan fumed as she stalked down the hall. *I'll show him what he can do with his fraggin' advice.* Everyone had told her that Lothan could be difficult, but she hadn't expected him to simply dismiss her. She knew the difference between professional discretion and a Mr. Johnson with something to hide, and Brickman was up to something. Lothan's refusal to even consider her point only reinforced her suspicions—and made her wonder about the magician's motivations, too.

She headed out the door, choosing not to slam it, and down the street. She wanted to walk, needed to clear her head before she decided what she was going to do next.

"Kellan, hang on a sec," a voice called from behind her. She turned to see Jackie Ozone coming down the street behind her. The decker now wore her jacket and had a stylish leather carrying case slung over her shoulder, which she steadied with one hand as she walked. Kellan stopped walking and waited for Jackie to catch up.

"You okay?" she asked and Kellan nodded.

"Yeah, fine."

"Don't let Lothan get to you," Jackie told her. "I'm sure you've heard the same advice from everyone else who knows him even slightly. What they may not have said is that he actually means well. The fact that he bothers to hand out advice at all means he cares, even if he's annoying the drek out of you when he does it."

"Yeah, something like that," Kellan replied with a snort.

"He makes a good point," Jackie began, raising a hand to head off Kellan's retort, "but I think you do, too. In my opinion, sometimes Lothan carries the whole 'professional courtesy and discretion' thing a little too far, and doesn't ask enough questions. Me, I'm willing to question anything and everyone, and my gut tells me your questions deserve an answer. If Brickman has an agenda that could come back and bite us, or that might be worth something to us, then we should check it out, right?"

Kellan smiled. "Exactly."

"In fact," Jackie mused, a slow smile spreading across her face. "It would be wrong of us to *not* check it out."

"Doing that is going to take a lot more Matrix muscle than I've got," Kellan said, lifting the bag containing her dataBook for emphasis.

"Well, then, you're in luck," Jackie said, patting the side of her own bag. "Since I happen to know someone with just the right tools for the job. Let's just see what Mr. Brickman is hiding, shall we?"

13

Kellan was surprised when Jackie made arrangements to check them into a coffin hotel on the outskirts of Bellevue. It was classier than the one Kellan stayed at. Not a haven for chipheads and other SINless, but the kind of place where cost-conscious business travelers caught a few hours of sleep between flights or after late nights at the office. When Kellan asked about it, Jackie explained that she hardly did any decking from home. With the existence of trace programs that could backtrack deckers' datatrails and locate them in the real world, Jackie preferred to not risk being caught at home.

On the way to the hotel, Kellan filled Jackie in on her suspicions. She described Orion's apparently tense conversation with Brickman at the meet, including Orion's mention of weapons. The decker listened carefully to everything Kellan had to say, apparently reserving judgment on what any of it might mean.

The clerk on duty at the coffin hotel did a double take at two young women renting a single unit. He leered, but didn't ask any questions as Jackie blithely slotted her credstick to pay for it, then took Kellan's hand to lead her to the elevator. Kellan could feel the back of her neck burning with an unaccustomed blush.

"Cover," Jackie said once the elevator doors closed. "All that twinkie is going to remember is two slags who wanted a crash-space together. He won't be wondering about anything else."

Sitting down on the foam padding inside the cubicle, Jackie unwound a collection of wires from a pocket of her carrying case.

"This your first Matrix run?" she asked Kellan.

"Well, in school . . ." Kellan began and Jackie shook her head.

"Nope, not school, or playing virtua-games with friends or drek like that—for real."

"Then, yeah, it is," Kellan replied reluctantly.

"Ah, a Matrix virgin," Jackie said with a smile. "Well, then, you're in for a fun ride. Here."

Jackie passed Kellan a collection of wires and leads connected to an elastic headband.

"You know how to use an electrode net?" she asked, and Kellan nodded. She slipped the band onto her head, adjusting it so that the electrodes made contact with the skin of her forehead and temples. They would translate electronic impulses into neural information and relay them directly to her brain. The resolution was a lot lower than you got from the direct mind-machine interface of a datajack, but Kellan didn't have a jack, so the trode net would have to suffice.

As Kellan settled the net in place, Jackie reached into her bag and removed a small, flat, rectangular object inside a burnished metal case. She set it reverently on the foam between them. Kellan let out a low whistle when she saw it.

"Nice deck," she said, and Jackie beamed with pride.

"Thanks," she replied.

"What kind is it?" Kellan asked, looking on both sides for a logo or brand name on the sleek casing. Jackie laughed.

"It's a custom build," she said. "Off-the-shelf is fine for newbies getting their start, but if you really want to run the Matrix, you need to know your deck inside and out. The best way to do that is build it yourself. This one has the casing of the old Cross Applied Technologies deck I started out with, but I've majorly upgraded most of the guts." She folded back the cyberdeck's protective case to reveal a sleek, flat alphanumeric keypad featuring a number of customized function keys. There was a slot along the side where a flatscreen rolled out, but Jackie didn't pull it out. The deck looked like a slim keyboard with slots for data chips and ports for plugging in peripherals, but no external display.

Jackie opened a side panel of the deck and un-reeled a thin fiber-optic cable with a standard jack terminator, which she slid into the chrome jack at her temple. It nestled there with a faint *snick*, lying almost flush against her head. The cable trailed down the side of her face. Then she took the jack for Kellan's trode net and plugged it into a secondary port on the deck. She powered up the deck with a tap on the keypad. Kellan felt a faint tingle as the cyberdeck initialized and its simsense circuits established contact with her nervous system.

"The hitcher rig," Jackie said, gesturing toward the trode net, "will feed you the same signal as me. It's filtered a bit, but you'll see, hear and feel everything I do in the Matrix. You won't have any control, though, that's all me. You okay with that?"

Kellan nodded. "Good. We'll be able to talk through the interface, but no backseat driving, okay? I need to stay focused, so don't interrupt unless I talk to you first." Again, Kellan nodded in acknowledgment, feeling a knot of nervousness and excitement in her stomach.

"All right, then," Jackie said. "What we know right now is that Brickman, our Mr. Johnson, works for Knight Errant and that he had some reason of his own for setting up our little run on Ares. He also has some kind of deal going with Orion and the Ancients, which may have gone sour, from what you told me about their conversation."

"There's the Street Deacon, too," Kellan said. At Jackie's quizzical look, she went on. "There was something about his expression when he saw Brickman, like he knew him or something, and didn't like him. I got the feeling it was mutual, but it's harder to tell with Brickman."

"Magical intuition?" Jackie asked with a raised eyebrow.

She shrugged. "I don't know. Call it a hunch."

"All right," the decker said. "So we've got Brickman, Orion and the Deacon, and something that might tie it all together. Sounds to me like Brickman is the center of all this, so we should check him out first. Since you already found something online, it's a good bet he's the most accessible, too. You ready to go?" Kellan nodded.

"Okay, get as comfortable as you can. This could take a little while." Kellan settled back against the padding on her side of the coffin, while Jackie did the same on the opposite side, their legs stretched out in the middle and the cyberdeck resting in Jackie's lap. Then Jackie tapped a key on the cyberdeck and the world vanished in a wash of silvery static.

Kellan fought down a surge of panic as she lost all sensation of her body for a moment. She was falling through an endless void of silent static. Then the chaos of static resolved itself into patterns and the world reformed around her in a different configuration.

Kellan found herself standing on a vast, dark plain under a night-black sky. Hovering overhead were constellations of orbiting neon shapes: cubes, spheres, stars, pillars and entire buildings floating there. Stretching off in all directions were glowing traceries of lines, with pulses of energy running along them at regular intervals. The horizon was a vast cityscape glowing against the darkness. Some of the structures were familiar—Kellan saw the Space Needle and the Aztechnology Pyramid—while others were completely alien, even impossible in the geography and physics of the ordinary world. They were in the depths of the Seattle Matrix.

"Still with me, Kellan?"

She started at the sound of Jackie's voice, seemingly coming out of nowhere.

"Yeah," she said, "yeah. Where are you?"

"Right here," the decker said with a laugh, and Kellan looked down to see one of her own hands waving. Then she realized: it wasn't *her* hand, it was Jackie's hand, or rather, the hand of Jackie's Matrix persona. The software in the cyberdeck created the illusion of a virtual world. It translated the information from the Matrix into neural impulses, sending them into the user's brain. That included the appearance of a "physical" self. It was like Kellan and Jackie were inhabiting the same virtual body, except Jackie was in control. Kellan was just along for the ride.

"Okay, hang on," Jackie said. She turned and stepped onto one of the glowing lines stretching toward the horizon.

It was like being on a roller coaster. Kellan felt as if she'd left her stomach behind as she suddenly zoomed along a silvery tunnel. Hundreds of other packets and bits of data flew back and forth in either direction, like a kind of digital rush hour. She changed direction, zooming this way and then that way.

Before Kellan even had a chance to get her bearings, it was over. The world snapped back into still focus and she stood out in front of a towering building. At least it *looked* like a building. The walls were of reddish stone, with inset windows of mirrored glass, tinted a coppery color.

"Welcome to the Ares Macrotechnology Seattle host system," Jackie said, imitating the stereotypical nasal monotone of a tour guide. "Ahead you'll see what passes for security at a secondary Ares site like this one."

Kellan could see the main doors of the building. Curled up on the wide stone landing in front of them was a massive black hound, as big as a troll. It had three heads, all lying on its folded paws, eyes closed. It was breathing slowly and deeply and appeared to be sleeping. Spiked iron collars around its necks were connected to a heavy chain bolted into the stone wall behind it.

"Standard Ares Cerberus ice," Jackie said. "Not terribly imaginative, but then, what can you expect?"

"Uh-huh," Kellan replied softly.

She'd heard of ice, decker slang for IC or Intrusion Countermeasures. Ice programs protected Matrix hosts from unauthorized intrusion, safeguarding the valuable data and systems within those hosts. Deckers specialized in finding various ways past ice to access that same data. The most sensitive data was protected by sophisticated ice. Most ice programs simply knocked a decker offline or denied her access to the host system, but Kellan knew there were ice programs that could trace a decker's location in the physical world, sending the information to the authorities or corporate security. Ice programs could damage a decker's cyberdeck, corrupting software or even frying the hardware. Then there was the legendary black ice, which could drive an intruder insane, or even kill a decker, inducing seizures or sending a lethal charge of electricity directly into the decker's brain. Kellan suddenly wished she'd asked Jackie how much protection the trode net afforded her.

"You don't have to whisper," the decker said in her mind. "It's not like anyone else can hear us."

"Oh, okay," Kellan said, somewhat sheepishly, in her normal tone of voice.

"Now, let's take care of Fido here." The slim, silvery-white hand of Jackie's persona reached out and plucked a large soup bone from the air with a flourish, like a magician producing a bouquet of flowers. She ran her other hand along its length and suddenly the bone split and there were three of them, held fanned between her hands.

"The triple-redundancy of the Cerberus ice is what makes it such a fraggin' pain," Jackie said. "But once you know about that, it's pretty easy to handle." She took a few steps closer to the sleeping hound and the middle head opened one eye to look at her. It snorted and all six eyes opened, its three heads rising up to look directly at her.

Jackie tossed the bones at the hound. They flipped end over end through the air, and the Cerberus neatly caught one in each of its mouths.

"There you go, boy," she said. The Cerberus immediately began gnawing on the virtual bones, hunkering down on the landing, its heads lowered. Kellan heard the sound of the dog's teeth grinding against the bones and shuddered a bit, but Jackie seemed pleased.

"That'll keep him busy for a while," she said, and then calmly slipped past the guardian hound.

"What did you do?"

"Modified a loop program that has it distracted," Jackie said. "I just had to make sure to take the redundancy of the ice into account. Now it'll be busy gnawing on that program for a while before it realizes there's nothing really there. I thought the bone was a nice touch, don't you?"

At the door of the building Jackie produced a key from somewhere in the folds of the flowing white dress her persona wore. She fit it into the lock and turned it to the right, and the door opened, allowing them to enter.

Inside the door was a foyer done in reddish marble and bronze, with a maze of corridors leading off from it in all directions. Jackie seemed to know where she was going, gliding along the corridors until they reached a certain doorway. The key granted them admittance once more, this time into a room filled with floating silvery spheres, row upon row of them. There were easily hundreds, if not thousands, arranged in perfect order.

"Personnel files," Jackie said, sliding along the rows. "Let's see what they have about our Mr. Brickman. Ah! Here he is." She stopped at one sphere and pressed her hand against it. Her hand sank into the surface of the sphere with a ripple like quicksilver.

Suddenly images unfolded before Kellan's eyes, displays with words and pictures scrolling down them. Jackie seemed to scan quickly through descriptions of Brickman's education and work background, skipping over pages of history to more recent entries in the file.

"Promotion to junior director of external resources and relations," she read out loud.

"Which means?" Kellan asked.

"It means that our Mr. Brickman is a professional Mr. Johnson. He handles shadow ops for Knight Errant, and he's up-and-coming, too, from the look of it. So it's not unusual for him to be hiring shadowrunners. He's not just a corporate suit playing a little game on the side. He works with runners a lot. Of course, that doesn't mean he *isn't* playing a little something on the side, but it makes it harder to tell.

"It might also be how the Street Deacon knows him," Jackie continued. She gestured and the file collapsed back into a sphere. With a wave of her hand, she brushed the sphere into the open mouth of a bag she held in her other hand.

"We'll just download this for future reference," she said to Kellan. The gesture told the host system to transfer the data to her cyberdeck's memory.

"Now what?" Kellan asked. "That didn't tell us much."

"I didn't think it would, but it's good to check out the basics. Targets rarely leave the good stuff just lying around where it's easy to find, but that first level of information is sometimes more revealing than it's intended to be. Most of the time, though, it's like diving for sunken treasure: it's a big ocean, so it helps if you know where to start looking, and you've got to watch out for sharks."

They stepped out of the room containing the personnel files and zoomed through the corridors. Kellan had no idea how Jackie knew where she was going. She certainly seemed familiar with the layout and defenses.

"Have you been here before?" she asked.

"Let's just say I know my way around the Ares system," Jackie replied, and Kellan left it at that.

They stopped just inside the entrance to a gigantic room. The ceiling was shrouded in darkness high above them, and on the floor below was laid out a collection of trucks, train cars, planes and even boats, all moving in complex patterns along a network of lines. Figures wearing plain coveralls marked with the helmeted Greek warrior of the Ares logo moved here and there, carrying boxes and crates, some of them impossibly large.

"Let's see what the shipping department has to tell us," Jackie said.

They approached one of the uniformed figures. Kellan saw that his badge indicated he was the foreman. He was ticking off items on a clipboard as other workers moved past him.

"I need information on a shipping route," Jackie requested, and the foreman didn't even look up from his work.

"Authorization?" he asked.

Jackie's persona reached into the folds of her gown, then opened her hand and blew a puff of glittering faerie dust over the foreman. It sparkled in the air for a moment and the foreman looked up from his clipboard, eyes wide, a silly smile fixed on his face.

"Works every time," Jackie said to Kellan.

"What did you do?"

"Used a spoof program that has the system convinced that we have executive access, for the time being." Then she withdrew a small, white business card and passed it to the foreman as her cyberdeck uploaded the search request to the host system. The foreman flipped through pages on his clipboard, then withdrew a similar card and passed it back to Jackie, who took it, downloading information to her deck.

The card in her hand expanded to become a floating window in the air in front of them. A map of the

Seattle area appeared on it, with routes traced out in different colors. Jackie and Kellan studied them for a moment.

"That shipping route Brickman gave us wasn't the original route for the shipment we nailed," Kellan stated. "It was changed."

"By Brickman, I imagine," Jackie replied, scrolling through the information on the various shipments.

"Look at this," the decker said. "There's an upcoming shipment that uses the same route." She traced the red line on the map with a virtual finger.

"In another couple of days," Kellan said. "What's in it?"

"Let's find out, shall we?" Jackie passed another information request to the foreman and he obediently complied, shuffling through his papers before passing a data card back to Jackie.

"Guns," Jackie and Kellan said simultaneously, after glancing at the cargo manifest.

"A *lot* of guns," Kellan added.

"It's a shipment for Knight Errant," Jackie said, "along with more run-of-the-mill stuff for Weapon World outlets in the plex. Now *this* would be something worth jacking."

"Hey," Kellan said, "G-Dogg said something about the Spikes having new weapons they obviously got from somewhere. Do you think there could be a connection?"

"Like?"

"Like maybe Brickman is setting up gangs in the plex with stolen Ares guns."

"Interesting thought," Jackie replied. "I'll do one more search, and then we should get going. I don't want to hang out any longer than we have to." She passed another data card to the foreman and Kellan felt an almost electric tension from Jackie's concern. Though the decker remained cool and calm, her desire to not linger in the Ares system made Kellan realize the potential danger.

The foreman shook his head. "Further authorization required," he said flatly.

"Damn," Jackie said. "The information is restricted."

"Can you get it?"

"Of course I can get it," Jackie replied, a bit peevishly. "It's just going to take a little longer." Suddenly, a glowing cloud of symbols appeared in the air between the outstretched hands of Jackie's persona, who began manipulating the symbols as if she were assembling a virtual jigsaw puzzle.

Kellan kept silent as the decker worked. She could imagine Jackie's fingers playing the keys of the cyberdeck like a musical instrument. The collection of symbols began to coalesce into a complex, multidimensional sigil. The sigil collapsed into the shape of a tiny data card, which Jackie passed to the foreman.

He glanced at it, nodded, and began looking through the papers on his clipboard.

A sound from the shadows high above the shipping area caught Kellan's attention. Jackie heard it, too. She glanced up, and Kellan could see a dark, winged shape come flying out of the shadows directly toward them.

"Jackie!" she said.

"I see it, I see it," the decker replied. She gestured, and suddenly her persona was covered in articulated metallic armor of chrome and ivory, from fine gauntlets to a helmet that Kellan could feel around her head, its widevisor allowing almost full normal vision. A slender silver sword appeared just as suddenly in the persona's hand.

The thing swooping down from above was a hideous mix of human and bat, with black, leathery wings stretched between narrow fingerlike bones, a black-furred body, whiplike tail, and a face that looked vaguely human but distorted with rage and hatred. Kellan had seen pictures of creatures like this: it was a harpy, or at least a virtual representation of one.

Jackie dodged to the side, narrowly evading the harpy's slashing claws as a hideous shriek filled the air. She slashed with her sword, but just missed the creature as it flew past, banking around for another pass at them. Jackie glanced at the foreman, who stood calmly shuffling his papers, as if nothing unusual was going on, then focused her attention on the harpy as it closed in for another attack.

"Ha!" she cried, slashing at the black monstrosity, but her battle cry turned into a yelp of pain as the harpy's claws raked across her left arm.

"Ow!" Kellan said as Jackie cursed. She *felt* that! It was as if a real harpy had cut her arm. Burning pain throbbed along Kellan's upper arm and shoulder. She tried to turn her head to see how bad it was, but it wasn't her head, and she couldn't move it. Jackie was in control of the persona and she was keeping track of the harpy.

"All right, you want to play it that way," Jackie muttered. She grabbed the edge of the white cloak she now wore along with her armor, sweeping it up in front of her with a flourish. The harpy banked sharply as it swooped in for its next attack. Confused, it hesitated for a moment. Then Jackie dropped the cloak and lunged forward, stabbing the thing with her blade. It recoiled with a screech.

Jackie spun and Kellan could see the foreman holding out a small data card. The decker lunged forward again and snatched the card from his hand, triggering a download to her cyberdeck.

"Hang on, Kellan!" she said. "We're out of here!"

They shot out of the room, and suddenly they were standing out in front of the building again. The Cerberus program got to its feet. The bones Jackie left it were nowhere to be seen. It bared its teeth and growled with all three heads, but Jackie just waved at it.

"Sorry, Fido, maybe some other time," she said. Then everything went black.

The light inside the sleep coffin was dim compared to the harsh silver and neon of the Matrix. Kellan blinked a few times and slowly moved her arms and legs, just getting used to the feeling of being able to move of her own volition again. She gingerly reached up and pulled off the trode net. On the other side of the cubical, Jackie sighed and opened her eyes. She reached up to pull the connector from her datajack, letting the inertial reel wind the cable back into the cyberdeck's housing.

"What was that?" Kellan asked Jackie, dropping the trode net on the padding. She reached up and massaged her left arm, where she still felt a twinge of pain. She looked, but saw no sign of injury from the harpy's virtual claws.

"I pushed things too far," the decker replied. "Put the system on internal alert and triggered an ice program. Nothing major, but I didn't want to hang around there and wait for it to get reinforcements."

Kellan shuddered. If that was what Jackie considered minor, she'd hate to see a serious threat in the Matrix.

"Will Ares know . . . ?" she began and Jackie shook her head.

"Don't worry about it. It was just an internal alert. The host system initiated some error checking and security procedures, that's all. It happens a lot, especially with corporate systems, so it's nothing to be concerned about. The system didn't alert anyone on the outside, and I made sure to wipe out all traces of our session when we logged off. So unless somebody goes through the system with a fine-tooth comb, there's no chance Ares will even know we were there."

"What did we get?" Kellan asked, recalling the data card Jackie grabbed right before they logged off.

The decker rolled out the screen of the cyberdeck and tapped a few keys. She shifted to the other side of the coffin so Kellan could see, too.

"Information on one other Ares weapons shipment that got hijacked a few weeks ago," she said. "The incident has been classified internally, but it looks like it was reported to Lone Star."

"That's weird," Kellan said. "Why report it to the cops and then classify it internally? Besides, I thought that Ares didn't like Lone Star?"

Jackie smiled. "Nobody *likes* Lone Star," she said, "but you've got a point. Ares usually handles this stuff internally. The megacorps have extraterritorial status, which means they're like countries unto themselves, and they take that status very seriously. They like to make noises as if they're cooperating with the local authorities; it makes for good PR, and this might just be more of the same. Except . . ."

"Except what?"

"The person who classified the earlier theft is none other than our own Simon Brickman."

"Again, why tell outsiders and then classify it internally?"

Jackie shrugged. "Maybe he needs to avoid an investigation from Ares higher-ups."

"Which means he's involved in the disappearance of those weapons."

"Good bet," the decker said.

"And that arms shipment went missing right before G-Dogg said the Spikes started showing up with new weapons," Kellan said, the pieces of the puzzle converging in her mind. "Brickman supplied them from the stolen shipment."

"Could be," Jackie replied. "I think it's interesting that Orion's gang, the Ancients, is currently at war with the Spikes."

"Which means Brickman is playing both sides of the street," Kellan said. "What does he hope to gain?"

"Apart from making a tidy profit from the sale of 'lost' weapons and getting two major gangs to wipe each other out?" Jackie asked. "Does he need another reason?"

"But then why supply both sides?" Kellan asked, and the decker shrugged.

"Double the profit, double the fun," she said. "Whatever his plan, it doesn't look like it affects us."

"What about Orion?" Kellan asked.

"What about him?"

"I think he should know about this."

"Do you really think he'll believe you, with no evidence to tie any of this together?" Jackie asked. "Do you think you owe him something?"

"I just don't like the idea of somebody I worked with getting played like that," she said stubbornly, and the decker couldn't restrain a small smile.

"Then you're in the wrong business, kid," she said.

Kellan bit back a retort. Even though she'd only worked with Orion that one time, he'd saved her life. He watched her back on the run, and she felt like she owed him the same.

"I need you to do one more thing for me, Jackie," she said and the decker raised an eyebrow in curiosity.

"Find out where Orion is."

14

The elves called the neighborhood *Tarislar*, which meant "remembrance" in their language. According to Jackie Ozone, Tarislar gained its name after February 7, 2039, the Night of Rage, when violence against metahumans exploded across the metroplex. The survivors found shelter in the lawless parts of the Barrens. Many elves established themselves among the abandoned strip malls and decaying condoplexes of the southern Puyallup Barrens, vowing never to deal with such small-minded, hateful creatures as humans ever again. Even some twenty years later, they did their best to keep that promise. Tarislar meant the elves remembered, and humans weren't welcome on their turf.

Jackie advised Kellan against going there, but when Kellan contacted Orion and told him she wanted to meet him, the elf insisted on the meet taking place on the outskirts of Ancients turf in the Barrens. So Kellan made her way to the place Orion described, an abandoned parking garage on the northern edge of Tarislar. It occurred to her for about the hundredth time as she walked up to the crumbling concrete structure that loomed over her head that she could be walking into a trap. She probably should have waited, tried to set up a meet in the daylight. As it was, there were few working streetlights in this part of the Barrens, and the darkening sky was overcast, reflecting some of the bright glow coming from the north. It was barely enough to see by, but Kellan made do.

The inside of the building had long since been stripped of any useful materials, leaving only some stained and battered countertops, and a large, dark concrete-floored garage. There were old signs of fire damage in places, and Kellan briefly wondered if it was the riots, or even the eruption of Mount Rainier during the Ghost Dance that caused it. The lava flats were well to the south and east, but she'd heard the fires had raged through the southern parts of Seattle for weeks.

There was no sign of anyone in the small booth at the entrance to the garage, so Kellan stepped into the dark, cavernous building.

"Orion?" she called out softly. Then she felt the

press of something cold and sharp along the side of her neck, and froze.

"All right," the elf ganger's voice was menacing, and close enough that Kellan could feel the heat of his breath on her neck. "You called me. I'm here. What do you want?"

"I want to talk," Kellan said, forcing her voice to remain calm, and keeping her hands clearly visible to show that she wasn't holding a weapon.

"I don't hang with your kind," Orion replied coldly.

"Look," Kellan said evenly, "I didn't come here to fight. If you're going to use that sword, then do it. Otherwise, put it away and I'll talk." She knew that she was taking a dangerous chance. There was a long pause. Then she felt the edge of the blade lift from her neck and heard the hiss of it sliding into its sheath.

"So talk," Orion said, and Kellan turned slowly to face him.

"Thanks," she replied, fighting the urge to run her hand across her neck to feel for blood. She kept her hands at her sides, maintaining the short distance between her and Orion.

"I didn't like the feel of the situation at the end of the run," she began cautiously. "So I've been doing some digging. I know about Brickman and Knight Errant."

The elf's eyes narrowed, and Kellan hurried to continue.

"I'm not trying to frag up your deal," she said, "but I think it's already fragged. Brickman is up to something."

"I don't know what you're talking about," Orion snapped, and he walked past Kellan to leave.

"I think Brickman is setting you up!" Kellan called after him, but the elf didn't stop. "He's selling weapons to the Spikes, too!"

That stopped Orion in his tracks. The elf warrior turned on his heel to look directly at Kellan.

"What did you say?"

"I said that Brickman is supplying weapons to the Spikes," she repeated. "He's playing both sides of the field and I think he's setting us all up."

Orion took a couple steps closer. "And how do you know this?" He folded his arms across his chest and waited.

"Like I said, I did some digging," she replied. "Brickman works for Knight Errant. He was able to get information on those Ares shipments because Knight Errant is an Ares subsidiary."

"Of course Brickman works for Knight Errant," Orion interrupted. "That's how we knew his offer was for real."

"His offer to set you up with weapons?" Kellan

asked, looking for confirmation, but Orion just waited.

"Look, I heard enough to know that the Ancients and Brickman had an agreement," she persisted.

"He was supposed to supply us with weapons," the ganger said grudgingly. "I assumed that was the run he hired you for, but that shipment turned out to be something else."

"That's why you were so surprised," Kellan said, "and why you were hacked off with Brickman."

"He claimed it was just a test run, that he had information on the real shipment and he would set it up so we could take it ourselves and keep the entire haul."

"Did that make sense to you?"

The elf shrugged gracefully. "No, but who the frag knows why corporate Johnsons like Brickman do things? I figured as long as we got what we needed . . ." Then he paused. "So what's this about Brickman supplying weapons to the Spikes? Do you have any proof?"

Kellan nodded and reached slowly into the pocket of her jacket to produce a data chip.

"This has info on a previous Ares weapons shipment that got hijacked before Brickman hired us, and probably before he contacted you. Ares supposedly doesn't know what happened to it, and neither does Lone Star, but from everything I've heard, it fits right in with the time the Spikes suddenly got some new toys and started fragging with the Ancients. The report has been classified—by Brickman."

She held the chip out to Orion, who took it from her, turning it over in his fingers, as if he was absorbing the data along with its implications.

"Even if that's all true," he said slowly, "you can't prove that the weapons ended up with the Spikes."

"I know," Kellan replied, "but it makes sense. The timing is right and those guns haven't shown up anywhere else. Doesn't seem like that kind of firepower would stay off the streets for very long."

Orion closed his fist on the data chip and tapped it against his lips as he thought things through.

"It makes sense," Kellan continued. "Ares 'loses' some weapons to a hijacking. They make sure to report it to Lone Star so it's officially recorded that the weapons are 'stolen.' Then Brickman puts the guns into the hands of one of the biggest gangs in the plex, knowing they'll use them as soon as they can. Then, when the Spikes cause trouble for you, Brickman makes you the same offer: he'll arrange for a shipment of guns to disappear, then hand them over to the Ancients so you can fight back against the Spikes. In the meantime, he hires some shadowrunners to do a test run and help establish a pattern of hijackings, maybe even set up someone else to take the blame when it all goes down."

Orion cocked his head, listening intently as Kellan raced ahead, the words spilling out of her.

"So then you and the Spikes go to war and pretty much wipe each other out with all the new guns. Gang violence in the plex goes through the roof, and then . . . and then Ares can step in and show how Lone Star isn't doing its job policing the metroplex! After all, they've let all these hijackings happen, and now there are gang wars galore. Knight Errant can make a real case for the metroplex police contract to be awarded to them when it comes up for renewal. And policing the Barrens will be that much easier once the Ancients and the Spikes and a few other gangs have wiped each other out in a big war."

"You're crazy," Orion said, shaking his head.

"You know I'm not," she replied. "C'mon! What's Brickman's angle? What's his cut when you get the weapons?" she asked and Orion shook his head.

"Nothing," he said.

"Exactly. So what's in it for him?"

"What's in it for *you?*" Orion countered. "Why are you even telling me this? I mean, you got paid. You did your job. You're not involved any more."

"I am if Brickman is using us to set up something like this," Kellan countered. "He used us to make his setup look convincing, and he may be planning to pin the blame for all this drek on us. I don't like playing the fall guy, and I don't like being used."

Orion snorted. "Get used to it," he said, echoing Jackie Ozone's words. "You're a shadowrunner. People use you."

"What about you?" Kellan asked. "Do you just let people use you? Because that's what's happening here, Orion, and you know it! Brickman is setting you up, plain and simple! He's using you! If you're okay with being someone else's puppet, then fine. I did what I needed to do." She turned and headed for the door, her steps loud in the darkened garage.

"Wait," Orion said, and Kellan turned to face him again. The elf ganger's expression had lost some of its arrogance. He opened his hand and looked at the data chip Kellan had given him.

"You're sure about this?"

"Dead sure."

"All right," the elf said. "You'd better be, because it's not me we have to convince."

"We?" Kellan asked.

"Yeah," Orion said, "if you meant what you said about not wanting to let Brickman pull this off."

"Yeah, I did."

"Okay, then there's somebody you need to talk to."

The leader of the Ancients was called Green Lucifer, and Kellan thought the name suited him. He was tall, even for an elf, all lean, tight muscle beneath the

205

street leathers and the torn T-shirt and jeans. His height and slender build were enhanced by a high Mohawk, dyed the same vivid green as the "A" logo splashed on the back of his jacket. He wore fingerless black leather gloves with chrome studs, and flexed his fingers like a cat extending its claws. Kellan had the impression of a caged beast, like a lion lounging at the head of his pride, licking his chops, but ready to spring in an instant. The predatory look in his dark eyes gave Kellan the shivers, though she did her best not to show it.

Orion managed to persuade the gang leader to at least listen to what Kellan had to say. She spelled out everything she and Jackie discovered in the Matrix and showed him the information on the data chip she had brought for Orion. She explained her theory of how Brickman was playing both ends against the middle, setting the two gangs up for a conflict that would benefit only Knight Errant and Ares in the long run. Green Lucifer listened carefully, taking it all in, giving her his complete attention.

When she finished, the elf gang leader leaned back in the swivel chair in the small office above the old warehouse the Ancients claimed as part of their turf. It reminded Kellan of a throne, and Green Lucifer was, in his own way, king of his particular part of the plex.

"So," he said in a surprisingly cultured voice, "tell

me what you think of all this, Orion." He raised one elegant eyebrow, pierced with a silver ring. Without even glancing at Kellan, Orion faced his leader, looking him right in the eye.

"I think she's right," Orion said. "Brickman is playing us, and we shouldn't trust him. This whole deal reeks."

"I see," Green Lucifer said. "And how would you suggest we deal with this situation?"

Orion seemed surprised that the leader of the Ancients was asking for his opinion. He thought for a moment before he replied.

"Get an explanation from Brickman," he said. "Find out the truth about what the frag is going on."

Green Lucifer nodded slowly. "Find out the truth . . . , " he repeated. He placed his hands on the arms of his chair and pushed himself up to stand, towering above the pair sitting opposite him.

"You're certainly very quick to believe the words of this . . . human," he said to Orion, throwing a glance in Kellan's direction. His intonation made the word sound like a curse, and Kellan drew herself up in her chair.

"She makes sense," Orion replied evenly, unbowed by his leader's scorn, "and I don't trust Brickman."

"As is right. But you trust her? Why is that, I wonder." Green Lucifer turned his back on the two of them, strolling behind his chair before turning toward them again, resting his hands on the back of the chair. He moved and spoke like an actor, Kellan thought, striding across a stage.

"Why is it," he repeated, "you suddenly decide this deal is a threat to us instead of the opportunity you considered it just a short while ago?"

Before Orion could reply, Kellan spoke up, standing to emphasize her point.

"I just *explained* that," she said. "Brickman is fraggin' playing you! He's setting you up!"

A look of incredulity passed over Green Lucifer's face, as if he couldn't believe this mere human girl was speaking to him in such a manner. His brows drew together in a frown, then a tight smile twisted his face and he laughed. It was a harsh, bitter sound, with no real humor in it.

"You poor girl," he said in a mocking tone. "Of *course* Brickman is playing his own game. So are we. So is everyone in the world." He spread his hands wide for emphasis. "It's the way of things. Do you really think that I blindly trust any human? Do you really think that the insights of some human child who has managed to evade her babysitter long enough to play at being a shadowrunner are of any use to me whatsoever?" He waved one hand in a dismissive gesture. "Go back to playing with your toys, little girl. I was making deals before you were even conceived. I know what I'm doing, and I don't need advice from the likes of you."

Kellan stood where she was, the blood draining from her face as Green Lucifer's sneering tone and words cut her to the bone. She clenched her fists and stared daggers at the gang leader, who met her glare with a mocking detachment that only fanned the flames of Kellan's anger. She felt the fire building within her, felt the tingling of the amulet at her throat as the magical forces simmered, just waiting for her call.

"Why, you stuck-up son of a . . . ," she muttered, taking a step forward. Then Orion's hand was on her arm and she whirled to face him.

"Not here," he said quietly, "not now," and Kellan swallowed an angry retort. He was right. She glared at Green Lucifer, who stood watching them, then she yanked her arm from Orion's grasp.

"As for you, Orion," Lucifer continued, as if there'd been no interruption in his monologue, "I would think very carefully before discussing your theories with anyone else—and I would choose my friends more carefully in the future."

"That's it?" Orion asked. "You're not going to do anything about this?"

Green Lucifer's eyes narrowed dangerously. "Are

you questioning my decision, Orion?'' he asked in a low tone, flicking the question like a whip. Orion didn't shrink from it.

"You're fraggin' right I am!'' he said fiercely. "You're talking about selling us out to a corp!''

The look on Lucifer's thin face was unreadable as the gang leader faced down Orion, who refused to look away. Then Lucifer smiled, sending a cold shiver down Kellan's spine.

"Very well,'' he said. He stepped around Orion to the door of the small office. Opening it, he strode out, heavy boots ringing on the metallic grate of the stairs bolted to the wall. Orion looked like he was in shock. Then, without a word, he set his jaw and turned to follow the Ancients' leader. Kellan wanted desperately to ask him what the frag was going on, but the look in Orion's eyes kept her quiet. She simply followed close behind him out the door.

Green Lucifer stood near the head of the stairs leading down to the floor of the warehouse. Spread out below him were a couple dozen elves in biker leathers, their hair shaved into Mohawks and dyed outrageous colors. A few of them played pool at a table on one side of the room, others lounged, or tinkered with the motorcycles lined up near the loading-bay door.

"It seems,'' Green Lucifer said in a tone that echoed in the open space of the warehouse, "that

Orion has a problem with the way that I choose to run things around here. Is that right, Orion?"

All eyes in the room went to where Orion and Kellan stood at the top of the stairs, and Kellan was suddenly aware of how quiet it had gotten. She held her breath, heart pounding, as the Ancients waited for Orion's response. She realized that Green Lucifer was giving Orion one more chance to change his mind, to admit his mistake and smooth things over. He looked across at Green Lucifer, not taking his eyes off the gang leader for a moment.

"That's right," he replied clearly. "I say you're selling us out."

Suddenly, the elves on the floor below moved as one, parting like leaves in the wind. Green Lucifer descended to the bottom of the staircase and moved out into the circle formed by the members of the gang.

"Stay on the stairs," Orion said to Kellan.

"Orion . . . ," she began.

"Stay on the stairs," he repeated, then he turned and walked slowly down the stairs. Kellan followed close behind, staying on the next to the last step as Orion stepped down and walked into the circle.

One of the Ancients held out a scabbarded sword to Green Lucifer. He grasped the hilt without taking his eyes off Orion and drew the blade from its sheath with a slither of steel on steel. The razor-sharp edge gleamed in the dim light of the room. Orion reached over his shoulder and slowly drew his own sword. Both men raised their blades in a ceremonial salute.

"*Li-ha?*" Green Lucifer asked Orion with a curl of his lip and the raise of a brow.

"*Sielle*," he replied, raising his sword in answer.

A moment of stillness hung over the room, and Kellan held her breath. An elven woman stood at the edge of the circle and raised a hand.

"*Akan!*" she said, her hand dropping.

There was a whoosh as Orion swept forward with his blade. Steel rang on steel as Green Lucifer blocked: high, low, then to the side. Then the gang leader came in at Orion and his blade flashed, blocking the incoming thrusts: one, two. They spun apart like dancers, facing each other.

They circled around each other warily, the first strikes just probing, testing the other's defenses. Orion lunged forward again, and Green Lucifer blocked. A sweep of his blade pushed Orion's aside, and he slashed. Orion ducked and his opponent's blade cut only empty air. He spun as he came back up and thrust, but Green Lucifer's blade whipped up to block again.

They circled. This time, Orion paused, letting Green Lucifer come at him. He ducked low to avoid a high swing, then leapt up and over, his opponent's blade passing beneath him. Kellan watched as Orion somersaulted over Green Lucifer's head to land on his feet right behind him. But the gang leader spun in time to block Orion's strike, their two blades momentarily locked together. Then Lucifer rolled back, dropping to the floor and planting a foot in Orion's stomach. With surprising strength, he heaved the other elf right over him, but Orion tucked into a roll and landed on his feet a short distance away as Green Lucifer came back up onto his feet to meet Orion's next lunge.

They circled and stalked in a rhythm punctuated by sudden flurries of attacks and blocks; the ringing of the swords, the slap of booted feet and the controlled, heavy breathing of the duelists the only sounds in the cavernous warehouse. Kellan's knuckles were white on the metal railing of the stairs as she watched. It was clear the two men were both masterful fighters, but Orion's posture and manner were deadly serious and Green Lucifer's face never lost its wicked, mocking expression.

It's like he's just playing with him. Green Lucifer took every opportunity to mock his foe with each move, every flourish of his blade, every expression, even in the way he stood. It was taking its toll on Orion. The younger elf came in each time with an attack more fierce and furious than the last, only to be repelled.

"Shata, goronagit!" Green Lucifer sneered, and Orion rushed at his opponent with a loud battle cry.

Both their blades were blurs of silver as Orion struck and Green Lucifer blocked, over and over, in the rhythm of the deadly dance.

Then the Ancients gang leader feinted. Orion dropped his guard for a moment. A swing came in too high and Green Lucifer's blade caught his. There was a twist, a flash of metal, and Orion's sword clattered onto the concrete floor a short distance away. Kellan's breath caught in her throat.

Green Lucifer's blade flashed and Orion cried out, dropping to one knee on the floor, a hand clutched to his face. Kellan could see blood dripping between Orion's fingers, gleaming wetly on the tip of Lucifer's sword.

Kellan didn't even think as she rushed into the circle, to where Orion knelt. Instead of striking a killing blow, Green Lucifer put up his sword, raising the blade before his face for a moment in salute, then swept it to point down and outward.

"*Carronasto,*" he said quietly.

Kellan knelt beside Orion, but he put a hand on her shoulder and pushed her away, rising slowly to his feet, his right hand still clutched to the side of his face. He stood and faced Green Lucifer in the middle of the circle.

"*Goronagee irenis,*" the Ancients' leader said flatly. As one, the assembled gang members standing in the circle turned to face away from where Orion stood.

Slowly, Orion walked over to where his sword lay. He picked it up with a bloody hand and slid it back into its sheath. Kellan saw now that Lucifer's sword had cut a bleeding gash along Orion's cheek; blood already staining his T-shirt red on one side.

Without another word, Orion turned and walked away from Green Lucifer, out of the circle of the gang members. Kellan glanced back at where the Ancients' leader stood, watching Orion go, with no trace of emotion on his face. The other elves were the same: like cold, beautiful statues. Kellan followed as Orion walked over to his Yamaha Rapier, mounted up and started the engine. With only a moment's hesitation, she climbed on behind him. Orion made no move to stop her.

He revved the engine and two of the gang members moved to open the door of the old warehouse. When it was open, Orion put the bike into gear and roared out into the night. Kellan glanced back at the tall figure of Green Lucifer standing framed in the doorway as it closed behind them, bloody sword still in his hand. She saw the elven gang leader's face twist into a bitter, mocking smile as they rode off.

15

Orion barely reacted as the street doc ran the surgical stapler along the gash on his cheek. Of course, she'd stuck a patch on the side of his neck providing enough beta-endorphin that Orion probably wouldn't have flinched at much of anything. He'd resisted the offer of anesthetic at first, but Dr. Falt insisted. "Or else I can't be responsible if I happen to stitch your mouth closed," she said. Orion didn't argue with her any further.

The elderly woman apparently knew Orion quite well and greeted him by name when he and Kellan went to her makeshift office in the basement of a building in Puyallup so Orion could get patched up. The street doc saw Orion immediately, ahead of two other patients. Fortunately, they didn't complain.

Dr. Falt must have been in her sixties, but her

gnarled hands were still deft, and her touch steady. She carefully closed up the cut on Orion's face, squinting at her work as she went.

"You're damn lucky," she said to Orion as she worked. "It's a clean cut and you got to me right away. If you manage to keep out of trouble for a little while, it shouldn't even leave much of a scar."

"Oh, it'll scar," Orion muttered. His mood had been grim since they left the Ancients' headquarters. He'd barely said two words to Kellan the whole time. Under the effects of the anesthetic, he was becoming a bit more talkative, though apparently no less depressed.

"Hold still," Dr. Falt demanded, grabbing Orion's chin and adjusting the angle of his head.

Kellan watched in silence as the doctor worked. Orion hadn't offered any explanation of what she had witnessed. She hadn't asked, but it was obvious it wasn't good. He'd challenged Green Lucifer and lost, and all based on what Kellan had told him. She felt responsible for his situation and wanted to do something to help, but all she could do was watch and wait.

In a few moments, Dr. Falt completed her work and looked it over with a satisfied "hmmm." She set the surgical stapler down on a nearby instrument tray and looked around.

"I'll get some spray bandage for that," she said. "Stay put, Tam, I'll be right back." Then she bustled out of the room and Orion laid his head back against the headrest of the chair with a heavy sigh, closing his eyes.

"Tam?" Kellan asked quietly, wondering if the elf ganger was drifting off to sleep.

"It's short for Tamlin," he said without opening his eyes. "A character from a poem my mother liked. He was a bard taken into faerie. She must have thought it was suitably elven."

"So your mother was an elf?"

"No," he muttered. "She was human. My father was an elf, though."

"Where are your parents now?"

"Dead. My father died in the Night of Rage, right before I was born.

"My mom raised me alone in Tarislar," Orion continued. "She was a doctor, like Christina," he nodded toward the door through which Dr. Falt had gone. "They worked together at the hospital. Some chipped-out punker in the ER shot her when I was thirteen. I've been on my own since then."

"I never knew my parents," Kellan said. "Only my aunt. My only memories are of living with her. She said my mother abandoned me after my father ran off and abandoned her, but I've never believed that. I think there is more to it than my aunt ever told me. She never really wanted me there, but she was all the family I had."

"The Ancients were my family," Orion said. "I joined up with a gang when I was fifteen, the Silent Ps. A gang is the best way to stay alive when you live in the Barrens. The Spikes wiped out our gang a few years later, when Lord Torgo took over. The Ancients kind of adopted the survivors. I was proud to be an Ancient."

"Tam . . . Can I call you that?"

The elf shrugged, which Kellan took as a yes.

"What happened back there?" she asked.

"The First Law," Tamlin said. "I questioned Green Lucifer's decision, challenged his judgment and his authority. That kind of thing has to be settled by a duel. I lost."

"So . . . now what?"

"Now nothing," the elf replied. "I lost. I'm not part of the Ancients anymore. I'm a *goronagee*—an outsider—not really even an elf anymore." He squeezed his eyes closed.

"I am so sorry," Kellan said. Orion slowly shook his head, his face relaxing as he sighed.

"Not your fault," he said. "I challenged, I lost. It's the way it is."

"Well, it fraggin' *sucks*."

Orion laughed weakly, then pushed himself up on his elbows, opening his eyes.

"*Sielle*," he said, looking at Kellan with his intense green eyes.

"What's that?"

"Yeah, it sucks," he replied with a chuckle. "Actually, it means, 'it is so' or 'it is the way of things.' It's hard to translate exactly."

"It's elvish, right?"

Orion nodded. "Yeah, Sperethiel."

"Do you speak it?"

"Not much," he replied, settling back against the padded chair. "Just a few words and phrases I've picked up. A lot of the Ancients like Lucifer speak it fluently, but they were mostly raised with it. My mom was a norm, and I didn't exactly go to school in the Land of Promise."

The Land of Promise. Orion meant Tir Tairngire, the elven homeland south of Seattle. It occupied most of what was once southern Washington state in the old United States, claimed in the negotiations after the Ghost Dance by a coalition of elves backed by other Awakened races and creatures. To Kellan, Tir Tairngire sounded like a mystical land of faerie, ruled by a Council of Princes and filled with magic and mystery. Kellan had wondered what it must be like to live in such a place, and why anyone would ever leave it. Still, there were young elves who came to Seattle from Tir Tairngire every year, apparently including some of the Ancients.

"Where'd you learn to fight like that?" Kellan asked.

"Mostly self-taught," he said. "I've got some Talent, too. I'm an adept."

"Like a magician?"

The elf shook his head slowly. "No. My magic is all in here." He tapped the fingers of his right hand against his chest. "It makes me stronger and faster—but apparently not fast enough." His hand moved toward his face, but fell back to the chair before he touched the cut.

"Sorry," Dr. Falt said, returning to the room. "You're not the only one who got involved in some foolishness tonight."

She used the canister of spray bandage to carefully apply a protective layer to the sutured cut on Orion's face. The transparent bandage molded to his face, barely visible.

"You'll metabolize the staples," she said, checking over her handiwork. "Just keep it clean and try to stay away from any other sharp objects in the meantime."

"Thanks, Tina," Orion said, getting up slowly from the chair. The doctor's businesslike demeanor softened a bit.

"Anytime, Tam, you know that. Is there anything else you need or—?" Orion cut her off with a shake of his head.

"No, thanks, not right now."

"Okay, you know where to find me."

As they left the clinic, Kellan, hands deep in the pockets of her jacket, turned to Orion.

"So now what?" she asked.

"Now nothing," Orion replied. "We tried talking sense. It didn't work. That's it."

"But you can't just give up!" Kellan said.

"Look, Kellan," the elf stopped and turned toward her. "I know you wanted to do the right thing, but it just doesn't matter anymore. The Ancients aren't going to listen. Whatever Brickman has planned is going to happen. We need to look out for ourselves, because it's sure as hell nobody else is going to do it." He gave a brief snort of laughter. "Maybe I can find work as a shadowrunner."

"Yeah," Kellan mused, "maybe you can, if you're up for it."

"What does that mean?"

"I've got an idea," she replied, taking her phone out of her pocket and flipping it open. "If G-Dogg is willing to do me a favor . . ."

Silver Max and Liada arrived at Underworld 93 at almost the same time. The club was open, but it was early so there weren't many people there yet. They made their way past Leif into the back room where Kellan, Orion and G-Dogg waited. When Liada saw Orion her eyes narrowed.

"What's he doing here?" she asked, lifting her chin in his direction.

"He's in on this," Kellan said simply. Orion kept silent as the elf mage and the dwarf sat down, Silver Max in an overstuffed chair that almost engulfed him, Liada on a smaller upholstered chair to the right of the couch where Kellan and G-Dogg sat. Orion remained standing, leaning on one end of the couch, arms folded across his chest.

"So who are we waiting for?" Liada asked, glancing around the room.

"Nobody," G-Dogg said. "We're all here."

"What about the Johnson?" Silver Max said.

"You're lookin' at her," the ork replied with a grin, inclining his head toward Kellan.

Liada laughed—a bright, musical sound, though Kellan found it grating at that moment. Then she stopped and glanced from G-Dogg to Kellan and back, an incredulous look on her face.

"You're serious," she said. G-Dogg just nodded and Kellan leaned forward, resting her elbows on her knees.

Here goes nothing.

"I've got a run, if you're interested."

"Just finished your first run in town and already you're setting 'em up," Silver Max said with a chuckle. "You sure don't waste any time, kid."

"You're wasting *our* time," Liada interjected, rising from her seat and picking up her shoulder bag. "I'm out of here."

"Hang on," Kellan said. "All I'm asking is for you to listen to what I've got to say. If you're not interested, that's fine. I'm sure there's plenty of other shadowrunners around willing to make some money."

Liada paused and looked at Kellan more carefully. She glanced over at Silver Max, who nodded slightly.

"Okay," she said, sinking back down into her seat. "You've got five minutes. Then I'm gone. What's this supposed run about?"

"Payback," Kellan said with a smile. She told the others what she'd discovered about Brickman and their run on the Ares shipment, and about her encounter with Green Lucifer and Orion's sudden departure from the Ancients, although she left out the details of the fight.

She explained what she suspected about Brickman selling weapons—or the routes of weapons shipments—to both the Spikes and the Ancients. She also showed them the data Jackie acquired from the Ares system.

"So what's this got to do with us?" Silver Max asked, and all eyes shifted back to Kellan.

"Simple," she replied. "I've got the information on the shipping route Mr. Johnson—Brickman—supplied, and Jackie has data from Ares about a shipment of weapons coming in along that route. The Ancients are set up to take that shipment, but we could hit it before they do."

"And what's in it for us?" the dwarf rigger persisted, though the tone of his voice said he was intrigued.

"The shipment," Kellan said. "It would be worth plenty to the right people—after we get first pick, of course."

Silver Max nodded sagely, his thick beard parting with a tight smile. Liada shook her head.

"Why should we cross Brickman, or the Ancients?" she asked. "That's a lot of potential trouble for just a shipment of guns."

G-Dogg spoke up before Kellan could answer. "You mean, aside from taking away Brickman's advantage over us?" The ork counted off reasons on his fingers, leaning forward and resting his elbow on one knee. "There's cred to be made off that shipment. Nobody's going to be expecting anyone else to go after it, since they figure nobody else knows. It hacks off the Ancients and, if we do it right, Brickman isn't even going to know it was us. The Ancients might, but I know how you feel about them, Liada."

The elven mage glanced at Orion for a moment before returning her attention to Kellan. "Who else is in on this?" she asked.

"Just us," Kellan said, "and Jackie Ozone. She

helped dig up the data and she can provide the Matrix overwatch, same as last time. Shouldn't be that hard—after all, we already did it once, right?"

"What about Lothan?" Liada asked. Her expression remained guarded, but Kellan figured that since she was still talking, she must be interested.

"He already made it clear that he didn't want anything to do with this," Kellan said, "but if you're not interested, Liada, we probably *will* need another mage. . . ."

The elf broke into a slow smile. "You really think that's going to make up my mind?" she asked.

"I don't know," Kellan said smiling back in spite of herself. "Depends on how willing you are to take a chance . . . and how much better than Lothan you think you can do the job."

There was a long pause as the two women regarded each other, then Liada grinned. "Well, since you put it that way," she said, "why not? I'm in."

"Me, too," Silver Max said and G-Dogg nodded, affirming his interest. Kellan looked around at the gathered shadowrunners, a combination of triumph and anxiety fighting inside her.

"Okay," she said, "here's what we're going to need to do. First, I think there's one other person we should talk to. . . ."

16

They found the Street Deacon sitting in his customary spot at Crusher 495 in Redmond. This time, Kellan went with both G-Dogg and Orion, the elf warrior insisting on being there for the meet. Same as last time, the Deacon didn't acknowledge the arrival of the shadowrunners as they approached him. He simply sat at the bar, nursing his drink.

G-Dogg offered to do the talking, but Kellan insisted on doing it herself. If she was putting this run together, she wasn't going to do it by halves.

"Deacon," she said. He showed no sign that he heard her. "I've got a job," Kellan continued.

"Find someone else to play with, kid," the Street Deacon replied, taking a sip of his drink, not even looking in Kellan's direction. "I'm not interested."

"I think you will be when you hear what it's about."

"Doubt it," the Deacon replied calmly.

Kellan forced herself to lean in closer. She put one hand on the bar in front of him, and spoke quietly so only the Deacon could hear her.

"I know what Brickman is up to," she said. "He's playing us all."

The Street Deacon turned to look at her, and Kellan forced herself to not flinch from the flat, dead gaze of his artificial eyes.

"Is that so? You don't even know half of what Brickman is about, little girl," he said.

"I know enough," Kellan replied firmly, straightening up. "I know he's setting up something between the Spikes and the Ancients, and I know he used us to test out a run to snatch some weapons, maybe even set us up to take the fall for the next hijacking."

"So? That's what guys like Brickman do."

"Now I'm giving you a chance to so something about it." The Deacon started to turn away from her, and Kellan said, "I didn't take you for a fall guy."

"I'm not," he sneered. "Not for Brickman, and not for you, either."

Kellan played her hunch. "Not anymore, anyway." The Street Deacon's attention snapped back to her with a look that made Kellan's blood run cold. She wondered for a moment if she'd pushed him too far.

"No," he said flatly. "Not anymore."

"Now's your chance to prove it to him." She paused, looking down at the bar, then met the Deacon's cold gaze again. " 'All it takes for evil to triumph is for good men to do nothing.' "

The street samurai just looked at Kellan, unblinking. Then he set his drink down on the bar.

"What's the run?" he asked.

As they left the Crusher, G-Dogg asked Kellan, "What was that you said to him? Is it from some book?"

Kellan shrugged. "Beats the frag out of me. Just something I saw in somebody's signature file online. Looks like it worked, though." G-Dogg grinned and nodded.

"You understand the Deacon better than I thought," the ork said, "though I think you were taking a real chance."

"I still don't understand why we need him," Orion said.

"Because we might need some extra muscle," Kellan replied, "and I've already learned it's better the devil you know."

G-Dogg gave her a tusky grin. "Nice to know you've been payin' attention, kid," he said.

They cut through the alley next to the Crusher to get to where they'd left G-Dogg's car. The roar of engines cut through the night, and the glare of motorcycle headlights stabbed down the alley. Kellan squinted against the sudden brightness, which rendered the bikes and their riders black silhouettes against the darkness.

"Hey, *makkaherenit*," a voice called out over the thrumming of the engines. "Green Lucifer sends his regards." The bike engines revved.

Orion turned to Kellan. "Go," he said, nodding his head toward the other end of the alley. "Now."

"I'm not going to just—" Kellan began, then the go-gangers drew their weapons and raced their bikes forward, like knights on eager steeds.

"Go!" Orion yelled, and G-Dogg grabbed Kellan's arm and dragged her toward the other end of the alley, just as two more bikes rounded the corner, cutting off their retreat.

"Aw, fraggit," G-Dogg muttered, reaching into his jacket and pulling Kellan toward the alley wall as the other two gangers roared toward them.

Orion stood his ground as the two bikes closed in on him. One of the elves whirled a length of heavy chain over his head and the other hefted a metal baseball bat, both of them laughing and hooting war cries.

In a blur of motion, Orion ran at one of the approaching motorcycles. He leapt up, his jump carrying him over the front wheel and handlebars of the compact bike, and planted one booted foot squarely in the chest of the elf with the baseball bat. The rider went flying off the bike, which hit the pavement and skidded sideways in a shower of sparks. The rider followed, hitting the ground with a thud. Orion landed on his feet and reached over his shoulder, drawing his sword in one smooth motion. The blade gleamed in the play of the headlights from the on-coming motorcycles.

G-Dogg, meanwhile, drew a heavy pistol from his jacket. He stepped out into the alley, spun toward one of the oncoming bikers, and fired two shots in rapid succession. The first sparked off the frame of the Yamaha Rapier, but the second was closer to the mark and took the rider in the shoulder. The impact almost knocked him off his bike, and caused it to veer toward the wall, forcing the rider to brake and skid to a halt.

Kellan reached for her own gun as the second rider roared past G-Dogg, headed for Orion. The elf war-rior dodged the chain-wielding ganger, who headed toward G-Dogg from the opposite direction. The two shadowrunners turned to meet their new opponents.

The whirling chain lashed out as G-Dogg turned, catching the ork upside the head. Kellan saw dark blood arc from where G-Dogg was hit as the biker roared past. Then she saw the other ganger G-Dogg had shot. He had regained control of his bike, and was drawing a flat-profile gun from underneath his jacket. Kellan spun toward him and snapped off a shot that ricocheted off the wall nearby. She successfully diverted the elf's attention from G-Dogg, but focused it on her. She dodged behind the club's trash barrels as the ganger fired off a couple of shots in her direction.

Orion turned as another ganger closed in on him. A heavy bat swung at the same time as Orion's sword flashed out. Sparks flew and the bat went tumbling end over end to clatter to the pavement a short distance away. The ganger looked dumbly at his empty hand as he rode past. The elf Orion knocked from his bike got back up and tackled him from behind. Caught off guard, Orion wasn't able to bring his sword to bear as the ganger slammed both of them against the wall.

The elf with the chain swerved in a squealing of tires, turning around for another pass at G-Dogg. He overestimated how much he'd hurt the ork, who raised his pistol and fired another two shots. Both of them slammed into the elf's chest, knocking him off his bike onto the ground and toppling the motorcycle.

Kellan popped up from behind the barrels and fired off another shot at the Ancient with the gun, but missed him again. She ducked as a couple more shots *whang*ed off the pavement close by. G-Dogg turned on the gun-wielding elf and fired a shot that forced the elf to abandon his bike and seek cover.

By now, the Ancients were dismounted, either knocked off their rides or on foot to maneuver in the tight confines of the alley. Orion grappled with one ganger as another closed in. A long, thin blade slid out of the back of the approaching Ancient's hand, extending out from his arm. It was flat black in the harsh glow of the headlights. Orion managed to push off the ganger and bring his sword up just in time to parry a slash from the Ancient's cyberspur. G-Dogg fired a couple more shots at the gun-toting Ancient, rushing across the alley to find some cover.

Momentarily safe behind the trash barrels, Kellan focused her attention on the elf fighting Orion. She concentrated like Lothan had taught her, feeling the flow of magic all around her. The now-familiar heat washed across her skin, tingling around her neck where the amulet rested. She raised her free hand and pointed at the elf, focusing, directing all the heat and energy toward him as he slashed and stabbed, and Orion twisted and parried.

"Burn," Kellan whispered, unleashing the energy she gathered. There was a rush of power as it left her, and a streak of fire cut across the alley. The elf ganger turned at the last moment, alerted by the sudden brightness, but too late to avoid the blast. The fire struck him square in the chest and there was a boom that shook the alley as flames exploded all around, engulfing not only the Ancient with the cyberspur, but his compatriot and Orion as well.

"Orion!" Kellan cried out. The flames cleared as thick black smoke boiled up toward the sky. The side of the wall and part of the pavement was blackened with it, and three figures lay on the ground. Kellan felt her heart stop when she saw it.

Heedless of the danger, she rushed out from cover toward where Orion lay. She vaguely heard the sounds of the other two elves retreating as quickly as they could, the bike engines roaring again as they took off, not wanting to face off against a spellcaster as well as G-Dogg.

Kellan reached Orion's side. His jacket and jeans were charred and burned in spots, and there were burns on his face, hands and parts of his torso, but his chest still rose and fell, and he groaned weakly and started to roll over as Kellan knelt by his side.

"Don't move," she said, placing as gentle a hand as she could on his shoulder. She looked at the other two elves lying nearby. The ganger she'd hit was clearly dead, burned to a crisp, while the other was burned like Orion, though it seemed like he caught more of the brunt of the blast.

Then G-Dogg was there, crouching beside her, looking things over with an experienced eye. He cupped Orion's head in one massive hand, looking at the burns on his face and lifting one eyelid to check his pupils.

"I think he'll be okay," the ork said, "but he needs a street doc or a healer." He turned to look at Kellan. "Can you do anything for him? Kellan?"

The request snapped Kellan out of the daze she was in. She glanced down at Orion, then back up at G-Dogg, shaking her head. "I don't know how," she said helplessly.

"Then we should get him to Liada," G-Dogg replied. "The Star will show up sooner or later, even in this part of the Barrens, especially when people start tossing fireballs around. Help me get him up." Kellan helped G-Dogg move Orion, though the brawny ork did most of the work. Soon, Orion was laid out across the backseat of G-Dogg's car. They drove away from Crusher 495 as sirens wailed in the distance, heralding the arrival of Lone Star. G-Dogg got on the phone as he drove. It was only then that Kellan noticed the blood oozing from a nasty gash along the side of his head, matting in the ork's dark dreadlocks. G-Dogg seemed to pay no attention to it.

"Liada," he said into the phone. "We ran into some trouble. We're going to need some patching up. Looks like the Ancients might be a problem."

Kellan was angry that Orion's surrogate family was trying to kill him, just because he was trying to do what he thought was right. She figured it was

Stephen Kenson

over when Orion lost the duel to Green Lucifer, but clearly the Ancients were not going to let it drop until Orion was dead. But she wondered, was dealing with Orion more important to them than their war with the Spikes?

"I think I know how to distract them," Kellan said, putting a hand on G-Dogg's arm.

17

Liada closed her eyes in concentration as she slowly rubbed her hands together, as if warming them. She whispered words in a soft singsong that sounded like elvish. Kellan saw a faint shimmering light gather around Liada's hands.

Orion lay on the couch in G-Dogg's apartment, his leather jacket tossed on the floor and the charred remains of his T-shirt lying close by. Liada gently laid her hands on him, one on Orion's forehead, and the other on his chest. She spoke a single, forceful word. Kellan felt the surge of magical energies, different this time than the kind of power she'd felt from the spells she'd experienced so far. It was gentler, soothing, almost a whisper.

The ripple of magic spread across Orion's body and, before Kellan's eyes, he began to heal. The angry red burns faded to a tender pink, and then to normal, pale flesh. Burned hair regrew along the side of Orion's scalp, and his chest suddenly swelled with a deep intake of breath, followed by a long, relaxed sigh.

Liada slumped over the elf warrior for a moment, catching herself with one hand against the back of the couch. As Orion stirred, she got slowly to her feet, brushing the long, dark hair out of her face and tucking it behind her pointed ears.

Orion's eyes fluttered open. He reached up and peeled the spray bandage off his face. The surgical staples and the cut were both gone, leaving only a thin, white scar behind. He ran his fingers over it, then across his chest where the burns had been. There was a look of wonder on his face as he glanced up at Liada leaning over him.

"Thanks," he said, and the elf mage nodded.

"No problem," she replied, sounding tired, but pleased. She turned toward Kellan and G-Dogg. "He'll be fine, but he should get some rest and eat something to help his body fully recover. Now, let me take a look at that cut, G-Dogg," she said, straightening up and moving over to the chair where the ork slouched.

"It's no big deal . . ." he began with a wave of his hand.

"Let me be the judge of that," Liada said crisply.

She parted the bloodied dreadlocks and appraised the oozing cut. Then she waved her fingers over the wound, whispering soft words. She gently pressed her hand against the side of the ork's head. When she lifted it away, the cut was gone, as if it had never been.

Liada puffed a tired sigh as G-Dogg brushed his blunt fingers across the side of his head.

"You can crash here for a while, if you want," he offered, and Liada nodded.

"Thanks, I think I will."

"Thanks, Liada," Kellan offered, glancing over at Orion. She couldn't believe that Liada had healed them both so quickly.

"All part of the service," the elf mage replied with a wave of her hand. "You toss a killer fireball."

"That's for sure," Orion muttered, levering himself up to a sitting position.

Kellan felt a hot flush across her face and neck as the memory of her blunder came flooding back.

"I—I'm really sorry," she fumbled for the words. "It was an accident."

"It's okay," Orion said. "You didn't mean any harm, and you sure as hell put an end to that fight. I'll just know next time to get out of the way." He smiled.

"If you're careful, there won't *be* a next time," Liada said in a firm tone. "You've clearly got power,

Kellan, but you need to learn how to control it. Until you do, I'd be careful about just throwing it around. Magic isn't a game and it's not a toy."

"I know that," Kellan said stiffly.

"Don't worry about it," Liada replied, her tone softening. "We all make mistakes. The first time I summoned a spirit . . . well, let's just say that I bit off more than I could chew. The trick is to learn from those mistakes. Don't try to take on too much before you're ready for it, okay?"

Kellan nodded. "Okay," she said.

"I dunno about you guys," G-Dogg interjected, "but I need some sack time and a shower. I get cranky if I don't get my beauty rest." The other shadowrunners wisely refrained from stating the obvious and found places to sleep.

Kellan volunteered to take the floor so the others could use the few pieces of furniture G-Dogg's doss boasted. She had certainly slept in worse places, and she felt so responsible for what had happened. If Orion hadn't managed to move when he did. . . . She pushed the thought aside. She would just have to be more careful in the future. She understood that magic was more than just an opportunity, it was also a responsibility. She just had to make sure there wouldn't be any more screwups.

Late the next morning, G-Dogg took them to a

local diner that served a hearty breakfast. They sat at a back corner booth, and G-Dogg ordered enough food for eight people. Kellan discovered she was hungrier than she thought, and the ork easily ate enough for two humans. Even Orion put away a surprising amount for someone so lithe. They tucked into stacks of soyjacks, accompanied by juice, soysages and plentiful amounts of coffee. Liada stuck with some fruit and a piece of toast, along with some juice. By the time they were close to finished, Kellan was feeling refreshed and invigorated.

"We can meet up tonight at Max's," G-Dogg said between bites of food. "He's got the transportation, and we'll want to go over everything once more before it goes down."

Kellan nodded in agreement. "Can you let the Deacon know?" she asked.

"No problem."

"Might be a good idea for you to lay low for the rest of the day," Kellan said to Orion, whose expression demonstrated he didn't care for the idea at all.

"Just until the run is over," Kellan pressed, speaking quietly, so as not to be overheard. "If the Ancients are looking for you . . ."

"I'm not going to hide," Orion said stubbornly.

"Last night isn't going to be the end of it, not by a long shot," G-Dogg interjected, taking a swig of his soykaf. "Every newbie in the Ancients looking to score some points and some street cred will be gunning for you, chummer."

"There's no point in making yourself into a target," Liada added. "You know this isn't over with the Ancients, especially if they think you know something that might be damaging to them. You're going to need to keep a low profile until the run anyway."

Orion sighed. "Yeah, I guess so."

"You can hang at my place," G-Dogg offered. "At least until things quiet down and you can set yourself up. Probably not a good idea for you to go back to your own place until then. You can bet the Ancients are watching it."

"Thanks," Orion said glumly, realizing the others were right.

Liada and Orion finished up and headed out the door, and G-Dogg turned to Kellan.

"Are you sure about having him in on this?" the ork asked.

"He *is* in on this," Kellan insisted, and G-Dogg held his hands up to ward off a tirade.

"I know, I know, but it could be trouble. As long as the Ancients are after him, he's going to be a target. And I don't want to go on a run with a big target on our team."

"If things work out, the Ancients won't be a problem," Kellan said, and explained her plan. G-Dogg looked dubious.

"You sure you want to do this?" he asked. "I can set up a meet for you, but it would be easier to just leave the elf at home and take our chances." Kellan glanced at Orion's retreating back as he mounted up his motorcycle outside the diner.

"Yeah," Kellan said, "I'm sure. So let's do it before I change my mind."

"So, anyone else feeling déjà vu?" Silver Max commented.

"Not exactly the same this time, Max," Jackie Ozone replied. "This time Kellan doesn't have to play bait."

"That's an improvement from my perspective," Kellan replied. "How's our target?"

"On its way." Max was observing the approaching shipment through the sensors of his drones. "Estimate three minutes."

"All set, guys?" Kellan asked, and G-Dogg and the Street Deacon responded.

"In place," the ork said.

"Ready," the street samurai replied in his laconic drawl.

The remainder of the three minutes seemed to crawl past. Kellan did her best to not wonder if she was doing the right thing. They'd gone over the plan multiple times, and they had the advantage of already having pulled off the run once before. How many shadowrunners got a test run for their jobs? Kellan had a hollow feeling in the pit of her stomach, wishing that they'd had more time, but in her heart she knew that no amount of planning could eliminate the uncertainty that came with running the shadows. Sooner or later, it was time to shut up and do the job.

"Here they come," Silver Max said curtly, and Kellan tensed. From the side of the road she could see the headlights of the trucks in the distance. There was a lead escort vehicle and the bigger cargo hauler following behind, exactly like before, the only difference being that this time the cargo truck was carrying a shipment of weapons and ammo, not cheap electronics. At least Kellan *hoped* it was the only difference.

The two trucks drew closer, headlights bright in comparison to the dimly lit stretch of highway. Two dull thumps sounded from the side of the road and the front tires of the escort truck blew out, sending the truck into a sidelong skid. The driver slammed on the brakes, red lights flashing as the truck skidded to a halt, and the cargo hauler's brakes squealed as it tried to avoid hitting the escort.

"Liada, now!" Kellan said over the comm.

On the other side of the road, not far from where

the Street Deacon crouched with the sniper rifle he had used to take out one of the truck's tires, Liada stood up just enough to get a clear view of the two trucks and the road. She raised her hands over her head and spoke the words of a spell. Ghostly light shimmered around her hands, and shaped itself into a dimly glowing sphere. Liada hurled the sphere of light at the two trucks as men spilled out of the escort vehicle's doors.

The sphere streaked into their midst and burst in a soundless explosion, a ripple spreading outward from the center to encompass both trucks. Kellan expected to see the guards collapse under the effects of Liada's stun spell. Instead, the faint shimmer of light seemed to reach its limit and rebound, snapping back into the center and winking out, like an ember blown out in the wind.

"They're protected!" Liada said over the comm. "Somebody blocked my spell! They've definitely got a magician with them."

"Fraggit," Kellan said. They'd considered the possibility, since Ares gave the last shipment they hijacked magical protection, but hoped Liada could end things with a single spell, and they could just move in and take the swag. Now they were going to have to do things the hard way.

"Let's move!" Kellan said, and the shadowrunners leapt into action. G-Dogg and the Street Deacon opened fire on the security personnel in the truck from their positions on either side of the highway. The guards scattered, one of them dropping to the pavement as a bullet got him in the head. Quickly, however, the Ares personnel recovered and began to return fire, looking for the source of the snipers attacking them.

One of Silver Max's drones, which had been keeping pace with the convoy, swooped down from behind the two trucks. Flying low, its engine whining, the drone skimmed over the top of the cargo truck and opened fire on the escort vehicle from the rear. The blast of machine-gun fire took out the two guards near the back of the truck, and half the remaining guards turned their attention to the new threat behind them.

Maybe this won't be so hard after all. Between Max's drone and G-Dogg and the Street Deacon, they could make short work of the guards. As if summoned by Kellan's thought, a shimmer appeared in the air above the cargo truck. A dull red glow sprang into being, growing brighter and brighter until a sphere of flame ignited, a crackling fire surrounding a shadowy shape. It lunged at Silver Max's hovering drone like a striking snake.

"Fire elemental!" Liada shouted. The elemental engulfed the lower part of the rotodrone in flames.

There was a hissing noise, and Max's voice, sounding labored, came over the link.

"Get this fraggin' thing off of me!"

Liada stood up again, pointing one hand at the fire elemental. She began to chant in a singsong voice, with a forceful, commanding tone. The fire spirit seemed to pause and Kellan got a better look at it; a sinuous reptilian form with dull red scales surrounded by a glowing aura of yellow-white fire.

The engine of Max's drone revved and it pulled away from the elemental, which hovered where it was, its attention fixed on Liada. She continued to chant. The commlink conveyed the strain in her voice.

The drone canted left before righting itself, smoke trailing from the armor plating on its lower hull.

"I've got some damage to the main gun," Max said. "It's jammed. I'm gonna have to pull back the drone."

"We need to speed things up, folks," Jackie Ozone urged. "Communications are scrambled, but the clock is ticking."

"Move on the cargo truck," the Street Deacon said to the others. "G-Dogg and I will cover you."

"All right," Kellan said, glancing at Orion, who nodded in response. "Let's do it."

As they moved forward, there was a howl of wind,

and a thick mist began to form in the air, coalescing near Max's drone. Kellan thought she saw a hint of a humanoid shape in the mist, with faintly glowing points of light for eyes.

"Fraggit," Silver Max said. "We've got another elemental! They're coming out of the fraggin' woodwork!"

As if responding to the dwarf's words, the road trembled. Something rose up out of the embankment in a shower of fragments of broken concrete and asphalt. It was a hulking figure the size of a troll, made up entirely of loose earth mixed with gravel, bits of concrete and glints of broken glass. It lumbered forward with ponderous steps that shook the ground.

"Keep going!" Orion said, giving Kellan a push toward the truck. "I'll keep it busy!" Then he advanced on the earth elemental, sword drawn.

Kellan kept going, staying low and heading for the rear of the cargo truck. Liada and the fire spirit were locked in magical combat, each stock-still and focused intently on the other. Silver Max's drone dodged and weaved as the air elemental buffeted it mercilessly with fierce gusts of wind, threatening to send it careening into the ground.

Orion rushed at the earth elemental, and it swung a massive fist. The elf ducked underneath it, replying with a slash of his sword. The blade cut deep into the elemental's body of rock and soil, leaving a long, ragged gash across its torso. The spirit howled a low, hollow sound, and raised its other fist to try to smash the small, dancing figure that had hurt it.

Ahead of the cargo hauler, the security guards hunkered down behind the escort vehicle, where G-Dogg and the Street Deacon tried to keep them pinned with cover fire from the sides of the road. The guards returned ineffectual fire—but it wasn't the two street samurai who were in danger. Kellan was worried that the guards would figure out that Liada and Orion were vulnerable, easy targets.

Things are coming apart. If we don't get out of here soon, we're fragged. She knew Jackie Ozone was handling things in the Matrix, jamming communications and rerouting emergency messages, but even she wasn't going to be able to cover their activities forever. The longer it took for them to subdue the guards and take off with the truck, the more likely it was the Ares personnel would get reinforcements or Lone Star would be there to take action.

The one good thing about the massive melee was that it provided an excellent distraction for Kellan. She approached the back of the truck as quickly as possible, staying low to the ground. Flattened against the back corner of the truck, pistol in hand, she listened for some indication of what was going on inside, but there was too much noise around her to be certain.

Bracing one foot against the rear bumper, she grabbed a tie-down strap with her free hand and hauled herself up, then she swung into the back of the truck, landing in a crouch and immediately covering the interior with her gun.

A human guard wearing an Ares uniform spun in her direction, looking startled. He'd probably been watching Orion fight the earth elemental through the slats of the truck, looking for a good opportunity to get a shot at the elven warrior. Kellan had the drop on him. She fired one shot at close range and took him out, his weapon clattering to the floor.

The noise attracted the attention of a hulking figure in the shadows at the front of the truck. Kellan knew this must be the mage commanding the elementals outside. He turned toward the sound of the shot and the guard falling. He wore a long, heavy overcoat covered with mystic symbols. He raised one hand, the other holding an ornately carved and decorated staff. He stopped just as suddenly as Kellan when the flickering light from the fire elemental hovering overhead illuminated the truck's interior.

"Lothan?" Kellan said.

"Why, Kellan, my dear, fancy meeting you here," the troll mage replied.

18

Kellan hesitated for a moment, at the sight of her teacher standing in the back of the truck, but Lothan didn't. Moving with surprising speed, the troll mage stepped forward and casually batted the gun out of Kellan's hand. It hit the side of one of the crates, clattering to the floor. Lothan seized Kellan by the neck, slamming her up against the side of a crate with enough force to knock the wind out of her.

"Sorry, kid," he said, with a note of true regret in his voice, "but hesitation in the shadows can be fatal." He raised the Staff of Candor-Brie, the crystal on top of it shimmering with an azure glow. Kellan squeezed her eyes shut and pictured the glowing, egg-shaped aura of protection around her. She felt a crackle of magical power tingle across her skin and opened her eyes to a look of shock and surprise on Lothan's face, quickly turning to annoyance.

"That cursed amulet. . . ." the troll muttered.

Then Kellan lashed out with her foot and kicked Lothan in the groin. Hard.

The troll mage gargled a noise a couple of octaves higher than Kellan would have thought possible and doubled over, loosening his grip on her neck. Kellan squirmed from Lothan's grasp and scrambled to scoop up her gun before turning back to where the troll lay gasping on the floor. She leveled the pistol at the back of Lothan's head and cocked it, confident he could hear it, before she spoke.

"If you even *think* of trying anything . . ." she began.

"I wouldn't . . . dream of it," Lothan gasped out, recovering his composure. The fact that he'd already tried something made it a dubious statement at best, but Kellan was more willing to trust Lothan with a gun trained on him than not.

"What the frag are you doing here?"

"Business, my dear," he replied, "just business."

"You knew," Kellan accused him. "You knew about this all along."

"Of *course* I knew! I'd arranged things well beforehand. I don't feel compelled to share every aspect of my business," the troll said condescendingly. "And neither, apparently, do you."

"Don't turn around," Kellan said, her voice cold,

as Lothan began to do so. The troll froze. "I may not be a 'master of the arts arcane,' but I do know enough to keep out of your line of sight."

"Well, you have an excellent teacher," Lothan said wryly.

"The elementals," Kellan replied curtly. "Get rid of them."

"Or . . . ?"

"Or I shoot you in the back of the fraggin' head! I'm not playing games here!"

Lothan paused for a moment and Kellan wondered if he was going to call her bluff. She wondered if she really *was* bluffing. If Lothan didn't do it, if he tried something, would she shoot him? The troll mage had certainly shown he couldn't be trusted. She knew he would take any opportunity and use it to his advantage. If Kellan wanted to survive, wanted to make it in the shadows, she was going to have to do the same. Her grip on the pistol tightened.

"No, I suppose you're not," Lothan said with a sigh. "Very well."

He slowly raised a hand, and Kellan kept a watchful eye on him the whole time, ready to react if he had some trick up his sleeve. Lothan called out words in a language Kellan didn't recognize, then turned his palm toward the ground and slowly lowered his hand, as if pressing something invisible toward the earth.

"They're gone," he said. "May I turn around now?"

Before Kellan could answer, Liada's voice sounded over the commlink.

"The spirits are gone!" she said. "We're clear to move in."

Kellan keyed her link. "Liada, can you use that stun spell to take out the rest of the guards?" she asked. "I'm sure we won't have any problems with it this time." She pitched her response so Lothan could hear it.

"Will do," the elf mage replied.

"Liada, eh?" Lothan said quietly. "I thought that spell seemed familiar. A pity she wasn't able to overcome my defenses." Kellan could hear the smug satisfaction in his voice.

"We've got to move things along, chummers," Silver Max said in Kellan's ear. "We're going to have company. The Ancients are on their way."

"Fraggit!" Kellan said. "How did they find us so fast?"

"They must have gotten tired of waiting for their pigeon to show up," the dwarf said, "and backtracked along the route to see what happened."

"How long?" Kellan asked.

"A few minutes."

"Sounds like you could use a little extra help,"

Lothan said, still facing away from Kellan. She ignored him for the moment.

"Okay, Max, take the wheel. G-Dogg, are we secure?"

"All clear," the ork said. "Liada's spell finished things off. The Ares guys are sleeping like babies."

"Get them to the side of the road and let's get the hell out of here," Kellan said.

"Roger that."

"Jackie?" she inquired.

"Things are under control on this end," the decker said. "If you get going now, there shouldn't be any trouble from Lone Star. I don't think Ares security or Knight Errant will be responding just yet, either, but it's possible that the Ancients may have alerted them when the truck didn't turn up as planned."

"Keep an eye out," Kellan said.

Orion rounded the back of the truck, sword in one hand and pistol in the other. He jumped onto the back of the cargo hauler with a single graceful leap, taking in the sight of Kellan standing there and Lothan getting to his feet. Kellan lowered her pistol when Orion arrived.

"What's he doing here?" Orion asked, nodding his head in the troll's direction, his brow furrowed with suspicion. Before Kellan could answer, Liada and the Street Deacon skidded to a halt at the back of the truck, just a few paces behind Orion, and the same question was written in Liada's expression. The Street Deacon's face remained as impassive and unreadable as ever.

"I thought that you might need some assistance," Lothan said before Kellan could speak up. He began dusting off his robe with one hand. "And a good thing, too, since I helped get rid of those deuced elementals."

Orion gave Liada a hand up into the back of the truck. "All of them at once, by yourself?" she asked, her tone incredulous. "However did you manage it?"

"Skill, my dear, pure skill," Lothan replied, completely unfazed. "Perhaps I'll explain it to you sometime."

"Max is up front," the Deacon said, ignoring the exchange as he pulled himself up onto the truck. "G-Dogg is riding shotgun."

"Okay," Kellan said. Only Orion had actually seen her pointing a gun at Lothan, and the elf seemed willing to follow her lead. If Lothan wanted to maintain the fiction that he was along to help out, Kellan was willing to let him. The troll mage might still know something helpful to them, and they weren't in the clear yet.

"Let's roll!" she said into the commlink and Silver Max fired up the engine of the cargo truck.

"Hang on back there," Max said, then he hit the

gas and the truck lurched forward and began to pick up speed.

"Um, Max?" Kellan asked. "Aren't we headed in the direction the Ancients are coming from?"

"That's why I said to hold on, kiddo," the dwarf rigger said with a laugh. "It's gonna be a bumpy ride." It was the most animated Kellan had ever heard Max, even more so than when he'd had a few at Dante's Inferno. It was clear that when he was driving, when his cyberware merged him with the machine, was when the dwarf really came alive.

They blasted past the escort truck. Kellan and the others held on to the straps and heavy metal D-rings holding down the cargo as the truck barreled along the lonely stretch of highway.

"How long to our exit, Max?" Kellan asked.

"Gonna be a few minutes."

"Will we get there before—?"

"No chance," the dwarf replied.

"Here they come," G-Dogg said, and Kellan could hear the roar of motorcycles approaching ahead of them.

"All right," whooped Silver Max, "who wants to play chicken?" He floored the gas and the truck picked up speed, rushing and rattling along the highway.

Kellan saw the motorcycles whiz past in the other lane. They were already slowing down. Clearly they'd seen their quarry, behind schedule but headed in the right direction. The elven bikers skidded to a halt and pulled U-turns in the middle of the highway. Kellan did a quick count; there were more than a dozen bikes, some of them with a couple elves mounted on them, but most with a single rider. Their engines roared again as they set off in pursuit of the truck.

"Liada, my dear," Lothan said, "since it is the Ancients we're dealing with, I think we should take precautions, don't you?" The elven mage nodded. Holding on to the cargo strap with on hand, she closed her eyes for a moment and waved a hand through the air. Lothan did much the same, standing closer to the end of the truck, and the stone at the end of his staff glowed faintly as he did so. Kellan felt a familiar tingle of magic in the air.

It was well timed, too, for no sooner was the spell cast than a crackling bolt of lightning erupted from the back of one of the bikes, lancing out at the truck. Kellan flinched and braced for the blast, but it never came. Instead, the lightning bolt seemed to strike an invisible wall scarcely a meter from the truck, splashing against it in a shower of blue-white sparks and dissipating with a crack of thunder, but doing no harm to the truck or its passengers.

"Harrumph," Lothan rumbled. "Strictly small-time," he told the others with a tone of disapproval.

"You should be able to handle the barrier spell on your own," he said to Liada.

"*Versoniel*," she replied in elvish. Kellan hadn't heard that word before, but from the look on Liada's face, she was sure it wasn't a compliment.

Lothan paid it no heed and instead turned his attention back to the Ancients. Gripping a handhold in one fist, he raised his staff with the other. He incanted in a deep and sonorous voice, weaving faintly glowing symbols in the air with the tip of the staff. Then he spoke a sharp word of command and pointed the staff toward the pavement. There was a crackle and a sheet of ice spread out across the highway behind them, as polished as a mirror.

Kellan expected to see the go-gangers go sliding in all directions when they hit the ice sheet but the ice turned into water before they reached it. The motorcycles sent up sheets of mist as they continued their pursuit.

"Strictly amateur, huh?" Liada called. Lothan, if he heard, made no comment. He simply lowered his bushy brows and frowned in concentration.

"Enough of this deviltry," the Street Deacon said, drawing his Ingram submachine gun from its holster. He fired a burst that sparked off the pavement and one of the Ancients' bikes. Then the gangers began to return fire, forcing the shadowrunners to duck for cover.

Orion fired several shots from his own pistol, but the back of the truck was swaying too much, and the elven bikers wove back and forth on the road behind them. The shots went wide.

Kellan heard several bullets *spang* off the metal framework of the truck.

"If they take out the tires, we're fragged!" Orion called.

Boom! Another blast of lightning arced toward the truck, only to be stopped short, but it was closer this time, and Kellan could feel the hairs on the back of her neck stand up from the electrical discharge. Liada's face was a study in fierce concentration. She was sweating, but also looked determined not to show any effort, particularly not after Lothan had dismissed the abilities of the Ancients' spellcaster.

Kellan stumbled a few steps forward to where the troll was standing, so she could get a shot at the gangers. Lothan had flatted against the side of the truck to make a smaller target, albeit only a slightly smaller one.

"Cover me," the troll mage said to Kellan, and she swung around him, firing off a few shots in the direction of the Ancients. The second lightning bolt had revealed the position of the sorceress, and Kellan tried to hit her. The Street Deacon let loose with another burst from his Ingram, and tagged one of the outriders, who jerked and fell from his bike. The Yamaha Rapier tumbled, then slid, and the rider did much the same.

Then Lothan lunged forward with a shout, pointing his staff at the Ancients. There was a surge of power that nearly knocked Kellan over—a barely visible ripple in the air, like a wave of heat—then a blast of green fire erupted along the edge of the highway, engulfing several of the riders at the edge of the pack. She heard a few screams. The remaining bikers emerged from the cloud of eldritch flame, but one cycle was without a rider, and tumbled a short distance before skidding to a stop. Three other bikes had disappeared altogether in the flames. Kellan saw them lying scattered across the road as the fire dissipated, and Lothan slumped against the side of the truck.

"Street-trained little dabbler," he panted, glaring in the direction of the unscathed elven sorceress. "Let's see how you match up with *that*."

Despite Lothan's display of power, the Ancients were not deterred. They opened fire again, and Orion and the Street Deacon laid down covering fire to keep the bikers dodging, prevent them from aiming, so their shots went wide. Kellan stayed down and fired off a few shots of her own.

"Remind me again what your plan was?" Lothan muttered sidelong to her.

"I wanted to keep the Ares guys from walking

into an ambush and getting slaughtered!" she said, popping up to fire off a couple shots, then ducking back down when her pistol clicked empty. She ejected the clip and grabbed another from the pocket of her vest, slamming it home and working the slide to chamber a new round.

"Oh, well, it seems to be going very nicely, then," the troll said dryly. Then he swung himself up, bracing himself with the handhold and pointing his staff at the bikers as he spoke a word of power. A bolt of lightning arced out and struck one elf square in the chest, blasting him off his bike. The lightning continued to play over the sleek racing bike, which erupted in an explosive *boom* as the spell touched off its fuel tank. Another biker was blown over by the force of the blast, the rest racing around the boiling black cloud of smoke.

"Mind telling me just what *your* plan was?" Kellan shot back at Lothan.

"Just here to help, my dear," he replied mildly, evading the subject.

"Max, how much longer?" Kellan said into her throat mic.

"Coming up!" the dwarf replied. "Everybody hang on!"

Kellan repeated Silver Max's warning to Lothan, but didn't heed it strongly enough herself. The dwarf rigger barely slowed down as he angled the cargo truck for the off-ramp, causing it to bounce and sway. Kellan lost her grip on the handhold and tumbled across the floor, trying to keep hold of her pistol. She managed to regain her feet at the very edge of the platform as the front of the truck hit the bottom of the exit and Kellan tilted backward, windmilling her arms.

Orion leapt forward and grabbed Kellan by the vest with one hand, holding on to a cargo strap with the other as they dangled over the pavement. He hauled her back into the truck as they hit the bottom of the ramp and tumbled toward the front of the truck. Kellan was dimly aware of a reddish light behind them as she scrabbled for a handhold along the wall.

"Take cover!" Liada yelled, and Kellan glanced back to see a massive ball of fire barreling down on the back of the truck. She instinctively closed her eyes and threw up a hand to shield herself as she heard Liada and Lothan call out. There was a roar and a wave of heat, but no more than opening an oven door. Kellan opened her eyes to see the reddish flames harmlessly dissipate all around the truck.

The remaining Ancients came roaring down the exit ramp in pursuit as the shadowrunners changed clips and readied for another assault. When the bikers reached the bottom of the ramp, there was a burst of gunfire. It ricocheted off the pavement and mowed down one of the elven gangers. Kellan glanced toward the Street Deacon, but saw that the samurai hadn't fired. None of the shadowrunners had.

When she looked back, she saw a collection of powerful Harley Scorpion motorcycles roar out of a side street, carrying nearly a dozen powerfully muscled troll riders. Each of them was armed with a heavy-caliber pistol or submachine gun, and they were firing on the Ancients.

Lothan levered himself up against the side of the truck again as the Ancients turned their attention toward the troll bike gang. He made a pass with one hand in front of him, then reached out as if plucking something out of the air with his thick fingers. A blue shimmer surrounded the Ancients' sorceress and she flew off the back of the bike, as if picked up by a giant invisible hand. She rose about four meters into the air and hung there, suspended, as the Rapiers of her fellow Ancients rode on. By the time the driver of her bike realized there was something amiss, he was a good twelve meters ahead.

Then as the sorceress shouted something Kellan couldn't make out and raised her hands, Lothan brought his hand down, palm flat toward the ground, and the elf woman dropped onto the street. She didn't even move before the heavy troll bikes roared right over her. Kellan closed her eyes tightly and tried to shut out the sound of her scream.

"Amateur," Lothan said with a derisive snort.

Without their spellcaster, and now trapped between two dangerous foes, the Ancients broke off their pursuit, veering onto one of the side streets. The troll bikers followed after them, showing the symbols on the backs of their jackets as they roared off in pursuit: a cartoonish image of an elf's head, with x-ed-out eyes and a spike driven through it.

"The Spikes!" Orion said, recognizing them instantly. "What the frag are they doing here?"

"I invited them," Kellan said. "I told them I had information that said the Ancients might show up around here about this time. I thought they might be able to provide us with a distraction, if we needed one."

"Well, I think they're doing a marvelous job," Lothan said, slumping against the side of the truck and sliding down to sit heavily on the floor with a sigh, leaning his head back and closing his eyes for a moment.

"How did you convince them?" Orion asked.

"G-Dogg set things up. We showed them a picture of Brickman, and told them it looked like he was cutting a deal with the Ancients. Apparently, Mr. Brickman *has* been working both sides of the street, supplying weapons to the Spikes and promising the same to the Ancients when the Spikes started wiping out their enemies. I figured the Spikes wouldn't care for being used any more than we did. I just didn't think it would turn into such a big mess," she said regretfully.

"Well, what did you think would happen?" Orion snorted, and Kellan shrugged.

"I don't know, that the Ancients would take off once things went sour, I guess. That they'd both realize they were being set up and they'd call things off."

"Maybe if it was anyone other than the Spikes," Orion replied ruefully, "but the Spikes have been our . . . have been the Ancients' enemies for way too long. It doesn't matter who's getting used or who's getting set up any more. It's blood for blood."

"Everybody okay back there?" G-Dogg said over the comm.

"Yeah, Dogg," Kellan replied, shaking off her other thoughts. They weren't done with business yet.

"Looks like the Spikes bought us what we needed. Great idea, kid. Max is headed for the drop-off so we can get off the streets."

"*So ka*," Kellan said. "Jackie, what's our status?"

"I think you're in the clear," the decker replied. "I'm going to massage a few things online to convince Lone Star this is just another outbreak of gang violence between the Spikes and the Ancients; their response will focus on the gangs, so we can use it as cover. Odds are Ares won't report anything to the Star in a hurry, if they bother to report it at all. Max is going to want to sweep the truck for tracers, like we talked about, but, other than that, it looks good. Oh, and I think I've got a buyer who's very interested in some quality Ares merchandise."

Kellan smiled and rubbed a dirty hand across her jaw. "Nice work," she said. "Set up a meet."

"Already taken care of," Jackie replied. "The buyer will join us at the stash site."

The cargo hauler clattered off into the darkened streets of the metroplex and Kellan listened to the roar of the bikes, and the sounds of gunfire, fading into the distance behind them. She glanced over at Orion. He was looking out into the dark, maybe thinking about the people who used to be his surrogate family. Were any of the Ancients who attacked them going to survive the night?

Her plan had worked, but at what cost?

19

Silver Max expertly guided the battered cargo truck through the back streets on the outskirts of Redmond, avoiding what little traffic there was at such an early hour. They'd chosen a different meeting site than before, but the new one was also in the Barrens: there were more than a few places in the Redmond Barrens to hide a truck, even one the size of an Ares cargo hauler.

The place used to be a mall, a retail store, or a commercial garage; it was difficult to tell for sure. The important thing was that it offered facilities to accommodate large trucks. G-Dogg jumped down from the cab to open up the overhead door and let Silver Max drive in, keeping an eye out for any signs of trouble. The shadowrunners in the back of the truck had been watching for signs of pursuit, but they saw none. The encounter with the Spikes had apparently sidetracked the Ancients, and there were no signs of Lone Star or Ares security.

Max left the truck's headlights on, since there was no other light in the room. They threw a glare against the wall, casting long, dark shadows into the corners. The light silhouetted a slim shape that approached the truck from the darkness.

"Right on time," Jackie Ozone said. "Are we all clear?"

"Looks like," G-Dogg said with a smile.

"Good." Jackie closed her eyes for a moment. As she dropped down from the back of the truck, Kellan could see the decker's lips moving slightly. She was subvocalizing, most likely for an implanted phone or commlink that was wired directly into her brain and linked to her ears and vocal cords.

Jackie opened her eyes with a small, satisfied smile.

"Our buyer will be here shortly," she said.

"Don't you suppose you should check to make sure you *actually* have the goods first?" Lothan asked, clambering down from the truck. All eyes fixed on him.

Kellan felt her heart sink for a moment before Lothan began chuckling, then laughing.

"Don't worry!" the troll mage said. "Just a little joke."

"Well, you would know what's really in those

crates, wouldn't you?'' Kellan muttered. Lothan's expression darkened.

"I know it may be costing me a fair amount," he replied quietly.

"Let's start with our percentage off the top," G-Dogg said. He began prying the tops off the crates, and Kellan suddenly got the feeling it was like Christmas for the shadowrunners. The Street Deacon acquired a pair of Ares Predators, the Mark III model, which brought a genuine smile to the samurai's pale face. G-Dogg, Silver Max and Orion each chose two weapons, and Orion held out a sleek new Ares Crusader machine pistol to Kellan.

"Check it out," he said.

Kellan took the weapon and hefted it. It was relatively light, with an extended clip and burst-fire mode. She sighted along its barrel. It was a top-of-the-line gun, and she decided to keep it.

"If you're quite finished playing," Lothan said dryly, "time is money."

"My sentiments exactly," said another voice, and Kellan turned to see a woman enter the building. She was human, wearing a smart corporate pantsuit and a pale blue T-shirt. Her straight blond hair was pulled back into a ponytail and she wore sunglasses, despite the fact that it was the middle of the night. Kellan assumed the shades either contained electronics and a heads-up display, or they concealed their guest's cybereyes.

She carried a slim bag slung over her shoulder, and a small, flatscreen personal secretary in one hand.

"Ms. Johnson," Jackie said by way of greeting, and the woman nodded.

"So, then, what do we have?" she asked, walking past the shadowrunners toward the back of the truck. G-Dogg gave her a hand up, and she quickly took inventory of the contents of the crates, excepting the items removed by the shadowrunners. She scanned the barcode affixed to the outside of each crate, then spent a few moments tapping the screen of her pocket secretary. Then she stepped down from the back of the truck.

"A nice little haul," she pronounced, heading over to Jackie and presenting her with the pocket comp. The decker glanced at the screen, then looked over at Kellan, raising her eyebrows in a silent question.

Kellan joined the two women, and Jackie held out the pocket secretary for her to examine. She looked at the figures highlighted on the screen and did her best to maintain a poker face. The truth was, she had no idea what the weapons were worth, though Jackie had provided an estimate beforehand based on the shipping manifest, which was pretty close to the figure the buyer was offering. She looked back at the decker and nodded slightly, and Jackie returned her nod, taking the pocket comp back from Kellan and handing it to the buyer.

"Done," she said and the woman looked satisfied.

"Very well. I'll take possession from here, then?" Jackie looked at Kellan, who shrugged.

"Fine by me," she said. "We're out of here."

Ms. Johnson slotted a credstick into the pocket secretary and manipulated the keys. There was an electronic purr, then she withdrew the stick and passed it to Kellan.

"Certified credit," the woman said, "as agreed. I believe that concludes our business. Nice working with you. Jackie, if you have other merchandise like this to unload sometime, let me know."

"Of course," the decker said with a smile.

The shadowrunners moved to the far side of the building, where Jackie and G-Dogg's cars and Orion's motorcycle waited.

"Kellan, a moment of your time, if I may?" Lothan asked, motioning Kellan over to him. She glanced at the other shadowrunners, particularly Orion, in what she hoped was a confident and encouraging way.

"I'll be right there," she said. Then she and Lothan moved away from the group before the troll mage spoke again.

"You don't have anything to worry about," he began. "I don't bear grudges. They're not very productive, for one thing. When you've been around as long as I have, you learn that it's better to focus on the productive side of things.

"I do also appreciate your . . . discretion in this matter," Lothan continued. Kellan could tell that it was a difficult admission for the old troll. "That you didn't say anything to the others."

"And I'm not going to," Kellan said, "though I'm sure they've pretty much figured it out."

"Of course—they're not fools. Well, not most of them, anyway," Lothan said quietly, with a faint smile playing at the edges of his mouth.

"But I'd like to know," Kellan said. "What *were* you doing, Lothan?"

The troll shrugged. "Like I said, just business. Our Mr. Johnson wanted a little extra insurance to make sure things went well. He passed me off to his people as additional security but, of course, I was supposed to help ensure that the shipment fell into the Ancients' hands."

"So you knew. I mean, when I came to you, you knew . . ."

"About Brickman's plans? For the most part."

"But you said . . ."

"I told you to stay out of it," Lothan said firmly. "With good reason. I didn't see a need to inform you of my business, since Mr. Johnson was paying for discretion. I thought it was enough to dissuade you, but I see now I should have been more . . . forthcoming."

"It would have saved a lot of trouble if you had just told me the truth."

Lothan smiled tightly. "If you're looking for the truth, you had best get used to disappointment, my dear. In my experience, few people ever tell the truth, unless it suits their purposes, and even then it's rarely the whole truth."

"You could have just trusted me," Kellan replied, and Lothan's face became very serious.

"Kellan," he said gravely. "If you never pay attention to any other lesson I give you, heed this one: trust yourself and your own instincts, but if you want to survive and prosper in the shadows, then trust no one else. Ever." Then the troll smiled, showing his tusks and yellowed teeth. "Except for me, of course. Trust your honored teacher and mentor in all things." Kellan returned the smile, but felt no warmth from it in the chill of the dark and empty room.

"So," she said, "next lesson on Friday?"

Lothan nodded. "I'm looking forward to it. I now believe your potential far surpasses my initial assessment. I suspect instructing you will prove a very interesting experience."

Lothan glanced over to see Orion approaching. He gave Kellan a parting nod, then turned and lumbered off toward the other shadowrunners. Orion watched Lothan go with a cool glance before turning his attention to Kellan.

"G-Dogg and the others want to grab a drink and something to eat before they head home," he said. "I'm going to take off, but I wanted to say goodbye."

"You're part of this team," Kellan said. "You should come with us."

"I don't know . . ." Orion hesitated. "I hadn't really thought about it until now, but I don't really have anywhere else to go."

"I'm sorry."

"For what?"

"For everything that happened," Kellan apologized, somewhat lamely. She hugged her arms to her chest, unwilling to look at Orion. "I didn't mean for things to turn out this way."

"I made my own choices," the elf replied. "I could have easily ignored you, gone along with what Green Lucifer wanted."

"Why didn't you?" she asked.

"I guess . . . because you cared enough to do what you thought was right," Orion replied. "You took a real chance coming to me with what you found out. Most shadowrunners just assume the Johnson is double-dealing then and accept it as the price of doing business. They don't think about what happens to people they don't know. You did, and that's pretty damn rare in this world, Kellan."

"Fat lot of good it did," Kellan said. "In the end, I just got a lot of people killed."

"I think that's why most people don't bother trying to do what's right." Orion frowned. "There are no guarantees it will turn out the way you expect. You can only do your best."

"I guess so," Kellan said. "G-Dogg and Lothan and the others make it sound like the right thing is whatever lets you survive and get ahead."

"Is that what you think?"

Kellan shook her head. "I don't know. Back in Kansas City, it seemed so simple. Seattle is . . . different. Nothing's easy here."

Orion shrugged. "My mom used to say, 'If it's easy, it's probably not worth doing.' You have to make your own choices."

Kellan looked at him and smiled. "Well, I'm sure of this," she said. "Right now, we're alive, we've got a hell of a lot of nuyen, the night's not over yet, and there's a whole metroplex I'd like to explore. It would be great if you came along."

Orion grinned. "You make me an offer I can't refuse."

Together they walked back to where G-Dogg, Liada and Silver Max waited.

"I made a call, and we can get into Reno's downtown if we move out now," G-Dogg said. "The door-man's a chummer of mine, and he owes me one."

"That's wiz," Kellan agreed. "Let's buzz."

She climbed onto the back of Orion's bike and hugged her arms around the elf's waist. G-Dogg took the others in the Argent. With a roar of engines, they disappeared into the shadows.

Epilogue

When the other runners were gone, Jackie Ozone went back into the abandoned building, where several men in nondescript street clothes had joined Ms. Johnson. They were in the process of transferring the crates from the back of the truck onto a flatbed, covering the barcodes and other markings with new labels, and even stripping the Ares cargo hauler. In a matter of hours, the truck would be broken down for parts. It was an efficient operation, but then Jackie expected nothing less.

"Your information was accurate," Ms. Johnson said to Jackie. "These Ares weapons will be quite useful, once we've arranged to put them into the right hands."

"I knew you would think so," the decker replied, and her corporate contact nodded.

"More importantly," Ms. Johnson said, "Ares will

end up with a great deal of explaining to do when the source of the weapons leaks to the media. I doubt they will 'lose' any more shipments of weapons in the immediate future."

"So much for making Knight Errant look good," Jackie said.

"Exactly."

"Lone Star's police services contract should be safe enough."

Ms. Johnson shrugged. "I couldn't care less about Lone Star," she said, "so long as Knight Errant doesn't acquire the police services contract for Seattle. Having an Ares subsidiary in charge of law enforcement here could potentially complicate matters for us. It's been trouble in Boston, and that's a good deal closer to our headquarters."

"So, then," Jackie said. "I can assume that everything is satisfactory?"

"Indeed," Ms. Johnson replied. She reached into her shoulder bag and withdrew a credstick, which she handed to Jackie. "Here's our agreed-upon finder's fee for setting things up." Jackie slotted the stick into a reader she produced from her own bag and confirmed the amount on it was correct.

"Excellent," she said with a smile. "A pleasure doing business with you, Eve, as always."

"Likewise, Jackie," the other woman replied. "I assume our arrangement remains just between us?"

"Of course. All the others know is that I found us a buyer for the merchandise in record time. They don't know anything about Cross Technologies' involvement or that I contacted you about acquiring the goods in advance of the run."

"Good," Eve said. "I would like to maintain our arrangement, if you're still interested. Having you on retainer has proven very useful to us."

"And to me," Jackie said.

"Good. Keep me informed of anything you come across that might be of interest to us, and I'll ensure you are well compensated."

"Absolutely," the decker said, patting the credstick stowed in her bag.

As she walked out of the building, Jackie saw a group of ragged gangers pull up outside, astride heavy motorcycles. The bikes were tricked out in red and orange flames, and each ganger wore a jacket painted with a snarling hound's head wreathed in flames.

Things are about to change along Route I-405, Jackie thought as she headed to her car. The Ares weapons would make the Hellhounds a force to be reckoned with in the area. The fact that the Hellhounds hated metahumans—especially gangs like the Ancients and the Spikes—would keep things interesting in the balance of power. She was sure that the fact that their turf ran near Knight Errant's training academy was no coincidence. She only wished that she could see the look on Brickman's face when he found out exactly where his missing weapons had gone.

Simon Brickman was clearly unhappy. He sat in his office, glowering at the two figures seated on the opposite side of his broad desk, his expression growing increasingly stormy as he listened to their recitals of everything that had happened the previous night, listened as the operation he'd planned came apart.

"Dammit, Lothan," he said finally, slamming a hand down on his desk. "What the frag am I paying you for?"

"You paid me to ensure the Ancients were dealt with," the troll mage replied calmly, "which I did. You *didn't* pay me to deal with unexpected trouble, or to throw myself in the way of danger."

"You certainly didn't have any trouble getting yourself *out* of danger," Brickman countered.

"I rarely do. Really, Simon, what did you expect me to do? Information leaked and we were caught off guard. I don't see how blame for that can be assigned to me."

"Oh, really? Strange coincidence then, that the shadowrunners involved in hijacking the weapons were the same ones you worked with on the first job, Lothan."

The troll mage turned with a look of disdain

toward the other man seated in front of Brickman's desk.

"Do you have something to say, Lucifer?" he asked.

"I think the implication is obvious," the Ancients' leader sneered.

"What? That I arranged to hijack the weapons away from your little band and sold them on the side for a tidy profit?" Lothan asked.

Brickman remained silent, but it was clear he had the same thought.

"Do you take me for a fool?" Lothan asked both men. "You know my reputation in this business. Why would I sacrifice it for the paltry profit of a shipment of guns?"

"Greed does strange things to people," Green Lucifer mused aloud.

"So does ambition," Lothan replied.

"Even if you were unaware of their plans, you should keep better control of your people," the elf said.

"I could say the same to you, since Orion was working right alongside the others."

"He's not part of the Ancients any more," Lucifer said flatly.

"Strange. I thought the intention was for him to be sacrificed along with the other troublemakers you were sending to their deaths," Lothan replied.

"Enough!" Brickman said, pressing his fingertips to his temples. "If the two of you want to fight over who's to blame, you can do it elsewhere. I don't have time for this drek."

"Fine with me," Lothan replied haughtily. "I only came to conclude our business."

Brickman slowly raised his head and turned to give the troll an icy stare. "Lothan, if you think I intend to pay you a single nuyen after the way this operation was botched, then you're more delusional about your own value than I guessed."

The troll returned Brickman's glare measure for measure. "I think I know my worth very well," he said evenly. "I know our agreement did not accommodate nonpayment for unforeseen circumstances."

Green Lucifer snorted derisively, but Lothan continued unabated.

"I will not accept breach of contract for circumstances beyond my control," he said. "I expect you to live up to your end of our agreement."

The two men glared at each other for a long moment before Brickman took a credstick out of the drawer of his desk and laid it on the polished glass top. He flicked it toward Lothan with one finger.

"That's as much as you're getting," the company man said. "Take it and be grateful you're getting anything at all."

Lothan stood, pocketing the credstick. "Always a

pleasure," he said with considerable sarcasm. "I hope your losses weren't too considerable," he said to Green Lucifer in the same tone. Then he turned imperiously on his heel and walked out of the room, the door closing behind him.

"Arrogant troglodyte." Green Lucifer stared at Brickman. "I can't believe you paid him anything for that debacle."

"Unfortunately, he's right," Brickman said. "With his reputation and visibility in Seattle, it's worth staying on his good side—for now. Just how bad *were* the losses?"

The gang leader dismissed the question with a wave of his hand. "Insignificant," he said. "They were expendable or else I wouldn't have sent them in the first place. I'd intended Orion to lead them. I hadn't expected his betrayal so soon, and especially not over some human girl." He leaned back in his chair as if it was his office and he was the one giving Brickman an audience, rather than the other way around.

"And what about our arrangement?" he asked the company man.

"It will take time to acquire additional weapons," Brickman mused, and the gang leader waved him off once more.

"The weapons are unimportant," he said. "I have other resources for acquiring what we need to deal with the Spikes, if they actually become a threat. I'm talking about our long-term goals."

"Those plans continue to move forward. I'll see to it you have the opportunity to expand your power base here in Seattle," Brickman said. "You'll get your chance at Tir Tairngire when the time comes."

"Good," Green Lucifer said, steepling his fingers. "Then this is just a minor setback. Orion is no longer a part of the Ancients, and I've gotten rid of a few other potential troublemakers, as planned, but there's still a great deal to be done. Ah, well," he said, dropping his hands to his knees, "patience is also a virtue." Then he gave Brickman a tight-lipped smile. "There will be other opportunities, after all."

Brickman nodded. "I'm glad we understand one another. I'll be in touch."

The gang leader stood and gave Brickman a slight nod of his head before turning and leaving the room. Once the door closed, Brickman leaned back in his chair and sighed.

"Well, *that* went well," came a voice from the shadows.

Brickman didn't react or even turn around at first, his fingers tracing idle patterns on the smooth desktop.

"Spare me the sarcasm, Midnight," he said to the empty air. "I've had about all I can take for one day."

A slim form in skintight synthleather stepped from

the shadows near the windows of Brickman's office, sliding the window closed behind her. She was tall, like most elves, her outfit hugging the curves and tight muscles of her lithe body. Her dark hair was pulled back, braided and coiled at the nape of her neck to keep it out of the way, emphasizing her pointed ears, her gracefully upswept brows and her large eyes. She had the cheekbones and lips of a classical statue, and her expression was just as hard and cold.

"How long were you listening?" Brickman asked.

"Long enough," she said. "What a waste. Having those weapons 'stolen' by the Ancients, then having Knight Errant move in to foil the theft would have been a nice double play. You escalate gang violence in the metroplex and make Lone Star look incompetent in the bargain. Then Knight Errant can step in to 'investigate' the other losses Ares has suffered and come down hard on the gangs, looking like the heroes."

"It's not a total loss," Brickman replied. "The theft will still create some negative PR for Lone Star. It'll need to be managed carefully, or else shadowrunners will start to think Ares is an easy target, and we can't have that. I suspect a few object lessons will need to be handed out to make it clear we're not to be trifled with. There's a fair amount of cleaning up I need done."

"I don't do windows, Brickman," she said, shaking her head, "or loose ends."

"I didn't call you here for that," he said. "I have something else in mind. Lothan is working with someone new, a girl he had with him at our meet. Green Lucifer said she was the one who convinced Orion to challenge him, and I'm certain she was involved in grabbing the weapons." He opened a drawer, pulled out a printout and tossed it on the desk.

"I want to know whatever there is to know about her. When I play a game, I like to know all the pieces on the board."

Midnight looked down at the picture, obviously taken covertly at the meeting between Brickman and the shadowrunners. She glanced over the features of the human girl looking into the camera. The youthful face framed in blond hair, the expression of bravado and inexperience combined were familiar, but her eyes were drawn immediately to the amulet the girl wore at her throat. Midnight picked up the photo and looked at it carefully, not daring to believe her eyes. But there it was, right there in front of her.

Swallowing her excitement, Midnight lowered the photo and gave Brickman a sly smile.

"I'll get you everything there is to know about her," she said. "It will be my pleasure."

ABOUT THE AUTHOR

Steve Kenson stepped into the shadows in 1997 with the *Awakenings* sourcebook. Since then, he has written or contributed to more than two dozen *Shadowrun™* RPG books. His first *Shadowrun* novel, *Technobabel*, was published in 1998. He has written three other *Shadowrun* novels (*Crossroads, Ragnarock,* and *The Burning Time*), in addition to *MechWarrior™* and *Crimson Skies™* novels. Steve lives in Merrimack, New Hampshire, with his partner, Christopher Penczak.

AVAILABLE JANUARY 2006

The next book in the ShadowRun trilogy:
SHADOWRUN™
Poison Agendas
by Stephen Kenson

Kellan Colt has been making a name for herself as one
of Seattle's up-and-coming shadowrunners, and she
believes she's ready to break out on her own.
Opportunity knocks when she learns the location of a
secret weapons cache abandoned by the U.S. military.
With the right buyer, a score this big has the potential to
secure Kellan's reputation—and her bank account.

With a team of fellow shadowrunners assisting her,
Kellan descends deep into the heart of the Awakened
wilderness to extract the weapons. But the supernatural
entities lurking in the forest become the least of her
worries when a rival faction appears seeking the
cache—and the greatest threat to them all is revealed.

0-451-46063-4

**Available wherever books are sold or at
penguin.com**

MECHWARRIOR: DARK AGE

A BATTLETECH® SERIES

R020

The first Parrish Plessis novel from
Marianne de Pierres

NYLON ANGEL

Bodyguard Parrish Plessis has just cut a
deal with a gang lord that could land her boss
in jail. She's also sheltering a suspect in the
murder of a news-grrl. In this world run by the
media, the truth isn't relevant, it's bad for
ratings. Now Parrish finds herself tagged for
murder—and up to her tricked-out leather
tank top in trouble.

0-451-46037-5

**Available wherever books are sold or at
penguin.com**

Penguin Group (USA) Online

What will you be reading tomorrow?

Tom Clancy, Patricia Cornwell, W.E.B. Griffin,
Nora Roberts, William Gibson, Robin Cook,
Brian Jacques, Catherine Coulter, Stephen King,
Dean Koontz, Ken Follett, Clive Cussler,
Eric Jerome Dickey, John Sandford,
Terry McMillan…

You'll find them all at
penguin.com

*Read excerpts and newsletters,
find tour schedules and reading group guides,
and enter contests.*

Subscribe to Penguin Group (USA) newsletters
and get an exclusive inside look
at exciting new titles and the authors you love
long before everyone else does.

PENGUIN GROUP (USA)
penguin.com/news